Old Mann Rock

Chelsea Lessard

PublishAmerica

Baltimore

First printing

ISBN: 1-4137-1421-8
PUBLISHED BY PUBLISHAMERICA, LLLP
www.publishamerica.com
Baltimore

Printed in the United States of America

Chapter 1

1872

Abby ran and ran. She only wanted to get away. Her father was a horrid man. He seemed to punish her differently than the rest of her sisters.

Abby was the middle child and was never paid much attention to. As soon as she did something wrong, Charles Cotter would get his black, leather whip out.

The only thing Abby paid attention to as she ran through the woods was the idea of where would she go? She didn't know.

Drops of wet pearls ran down her face, and then stained her face with redness. Rushing water was what she suddenly heard. As she came closer and closer, she realized, above all the grief she was feeling, there was the most beautiful river.

She gasped in astonishment. She could not believe her very eyes. Was she dreaming? The river was like a crystal clear blanket, with pebbles drawn in the background. It wasn't very wide, but was perfect.

Suddenly she heard a strange noise.

She turned around to see what it was. A boy, maybe a few years older than her, stood there in rags.

He was tall for his age. Dust and filth covered his face. His hair was snarled. He wore navy blue trousers, which had holes in the knees. He did not wear a shirt, and he looked strong.

"Hello," Abby said, holding her hand out.

"Hi," he replied. He was mysterious in a sort of rebellious way. He walked to the edge of the riverbank, and then looked back at Abby. "I'm Billy." He shook her hand in a proper meeting.

"I am Abigail Cotter," she sniffled.

Billy looked at her closely and frowned. "Have you been crying?" Abby turned in embarrassment and placed her hands over her face to cry more. "What's wrong?" He tried to reassure her by planting his hand on her shoulder.

Abby turned again, "Nothing." She wiped her tears away. "I'm fine, thank you." His hand did reassure her and she smiled. "Is that your canoe?" she said calmly.

"It is," he answered. "Can I show you something?" He got into the canoe and held out his hand. Abby kindly was led into the boat and she sat on the seat, which was waiting for her. "This will cheer you up," he told her. "It always cheers me up when I'm having a bad day like you are having today."

Billy took his long pole and pushed off shore. "It's a lovely river," she added. "I never knew it lay here."

"It's my home," Billy told her.

"Really?" she asked in envy. "I would love to live here. What about your parents? Isn't it too much trouble to go into town?" Billy's face became a frown of sadness. "Oh!" Her curiosity had hurt him, she realized. "I'm so sorry."

"I'm an orphan. I live on the river alone, ever since I was nine years old," Billy said still calm. He put his pole in the canoe and let them drift off.

"How old are you now?" Abby asked.

"I'm twelve, I think," he replied.

"I am ten. I could not imagine living by myself for so long."

"It's nothing really," he added.

"Although I am lonely most of the time, I still couldn't imagine it," she told him.

"I do get lonely, that's true."

"Why don't you go to the orphanage in town?" she asked with curiosity. "You won't be lonely there." He started to row with his long pole again.

"Because Old Mann Rock is my home," he replied.

"What is Old Mann Rock?" she questioned.

"This," he replied once again. It was the loveliest sight she had ever seen. The river was wider at this part. Sunlight poured from the deep blue sky and swallowed her up in amazement.

Had she died and gone to heaven?

Birds flew and chirped in happiness. This was truly paradise. "I call it Old Mann Rock because, you see," he pointed to the gigantic rock which protected this paradise. "It looks like an old man. This actually is my father's property. That's what its name really is. Since he died, the land is mine."

"It's beautiful, Billy," she added as she looked around again in awe. A rope was tied around a branch, which hung from an old oak tree over the boulder. "What is that rope for?"

"To swing off, of course." Billy rowed them to the shore next to the old man. "Wanna go?"

"I'm scared," she admitted.

"Don't be," he told her. "I'll go first." Billy stepped on the high rock and took a branch perfect to fetch the rope to him. The limb hooked around the worn rope and was then in his hands. "Here I go," he warned her. Billy leapt off the rock. Abby thought he looked like he was flying. He let go of the rope when it was far out in the air as it could go. A splash of water was made when he went into it, like a pin that dropped on the ground only louder. Billy's head popped up only seconds after.

"Abigail, you try now." He climbed out of the water on shore and led Abby to the rock. Again, he fetched the rope with his branch, but gave it to her this time.

Abby swallowed hard and took a glimpse at Billy. "Here I go." Abby was unsure if she wanted to. She closed her eyes tight and jumped off. Now she felt like she was flying. She opened her eyes and let go of the rope. She held her breath when she went under and bobbed back up like a toy sailboat in a child's bathtub.

She loved it.

Darkness fell over the sky and Billy lit a fire next to the rock. "Could I come back tomorrow?" she wondered.

"Sure," he told her. Abby sighed; it was the most fun she had had in a long time.

"Thank you for bringing me here. Tomorrow, I'll meet you where we met today. I should get back now. How do you get out of here?" she asked him.

"I'll take you back. The river circles the town, so we go around to get back."

They both went in the well-made boat and said nothing. Abby was sad the day had ended, but somehow she knew it wouldn't be the last.

When the bank of her stop came, Billy set the pole to go on shore. He helped her out. "I'll see you tomorrow, Abigail."

"Oh! You can call me Abby."

"All right, I'll see you tomorrow, Abby. Good night."

"Good night." She turned around smiling. Still drenched, she walked toward her home.

Billy watched her walk away. He knew a friendship had started to form. Billy thought she was beautiful. Her hair was black and long. Her eyes twinkled in the moonlight like they were stars themselves. He could not wait for the next day.

He knew he would not be alone anymore.

Chapter 2

September 1877

The Cotter family sat at the dining table saying prayer. When the prayer was over, food was eaten and not a word was spoken. The rule was, no talking until Father did. Abby hated breakfast because it always delayed her from going to Old Mann Rock.

The breakfast was wordless. It was silent. Abby observed everyone's face. Everyone was doing the same as she was, except her father. It didn't matter to Abby because she said nothing at breakfast anyway. She ate her breakfast fast and was done before anyone was half done. Abby wished she had not eaten so fast because she had to wait for them to finish.

The windows were slightly opened, but were opened wide enough to welcome the wind inside. It was a nice breeze. It went well with the blue sky. Abby thought about what they would do today, as she sat there waiting.

Then her father stood up and left.

When he left, it meant everyone else could too. Abby helped her mother with the dishes. Not that she wanted to.

After she was done, she ran to her bedroom. Abby wore the same dress everyday to Old Mann Rock. It was quite dirty. Today she wore a different dress because it was much cooler than yesterday.

Winter was coming, she knew. The foliage of New England covered the trees, which gave the secret away. Fall was Abby's favorite season because of the beauty of the nature.

During fall, instead of running through the woods, she would stroll. Abby would look at the different shades of magnificent colors as she looked at the tall, overbearing trees.

She did just that today. When she got to the river, sure enough, Billy was waiting there for her. He always knew why she was late this time of year. It didn't bother him. He would always bring something to carve. Billy was always carving something out of wood with his sharp-edged butcher knife. He would always make Abby things such as flutes, boxes, and toys. Sure, Abby was a little too old to play with toys, but she treasured them and Billy knew it. When Abby was ten, Billy made her a doll and clothed it with his mother's clothes from her old dolls.

"What are you making today?"

Billy looked up at Abby on the bank. He knew she wore a new dress and thought she looked lovely in it. "It's part of your Christmas present," he told her.

"You don't care if I see it?" she asked confused over the matter.

"It's just a little part," he added as he stood up to help Abby in the boat.

"Christmas is far away," she reminded him as she sat down.

Billy pushed off the bank. "I know, but it's a big gift."

She wondered what it was. "Okay."

What was she going to give him? Ever since they knew each other, they always gave each other presents.

"I am actually giving you two," he teased.

"What? Why? You really don't need to…"

He interrupted her sentence. "Believe me, one is what I should have given you a while ago."

Abby would always steal her gifts for Billy from her father's general store he owned on the corner of Main Street and Fryeburg Lane. It didn't bother her at all because stealing from her father was a joy. He deserved it. Billy deserved the best and she always gave it to him. Last year, she stole a knife sharpener for his butcher knife. Billy absolutely loved it.

She would get him new clothing, she thought as Billy poled down the river. She would get him new shoes, new pants and a new shirt all from Boston. Her father always ordered the best from Boston.

Billy broke her concentration. "I have a surprise to show you."

"A surprise? What is the occasion?" she questioned the second her eyes lit up.

"No occasion," he replied. "Just is something I have wanted to show you for a long time."

What could it be? There were so many things Abby knew Billy kept from her. She never did mind it much. "What is it?"

"Just you wait," he chuckled. "Abigail Cotter, I think you are the worst when it comes to surprises!" he teased as he waved his hand in the air as if he was addressing the river.

She giggled. "Maybe I am, but that does not make you any better."

"Right," he admitted. Abby's black as night eyes twinkled in the sunlight from laughing so much as she looked up at him.

She smiled. "My God, seems like Old Mann Rock is much farther away today."

"It's only because you know there's a surprise waiting for you there. I must tell you, I hope you won't be disappointed. It isn't much."

"I always love your surprises, Billy."

Finally, they reached their destination at Old Mann Rock.

Billy anchored the boat and Abby looked around to see the gift that Billy had been hiding from her. She saw nothing.

What could it be?

"Follow me," he demanded, kindly.

Abby obeyed and she followed him to a path that led to the woods. It was a well-hidden path, which was no more than two feet wide.

Where were they going?

It was about a quarter of a mile when she saw it. It was large and grand. Made out of fine wooden logs, it stood two stories.

His house!

Why didn't she think of that? Billy had never shown her where he lived. It was lovely. Her expression on her face spoke all the words. Billy knew she loved it. Abby's eyes grew big and they smiled.

"You live here?" she awed.

"I do. Beautiful, isn't it? My father built it when my mother was in child with me." Flowers bloomed as if it was the beginning of the summer. Great oak and maple trees guarded the house with its long branches as if it were a child hugging its teddy bear tight.

"Could we go inside?" her curiosity had exploded.

Billy nodded and climbed the few steps that led to the covered porch. He opened the heavy oak door. Inside was beautiful. The wood was fine-detailed. It looked like a palace. Billy directed her to the parlor. Beautiful furniture, as if they were in Boston themselves, made the room spectacular. The huge fireplace stood against the wall in perfect order. Delightful lace curtains hung over the windowpanes. A European area rug hovered the wooden floor. Portraits of beautiful people were placed with care on the walls.

The kitchen had a wood stove with another fireplace. The fireplace consisted of two gigantic ovens and a brick hearth. Big, black iron kettles hung on nails, which were cemented into the stone on the fireplace. A small icebox was placed in the corner.

The dining area had a great oak table. Eight elegant chairs in straight lines were edged along the table. A brilliant bouquet of radiant colors was in the center. The petals appeared like silk and looked as if they were freshly picked yesterday.

Billy walked over to an oak door, not as heavy as the front door, and opened it. Inside, were books.

A library!

Every wall was covered with different color bindings of the books stacked on the shelves. In the center of the room, lay another European rug and two chairs around a wooden table.

Abby grinned. "Wow!"

"Do you read?" a surprised tone was in his voice.

"I do. Do you?"

"Nah," he shrugged, "I never had the time."

"Oh, well reading is lovely. Reading takes you places you've never been before and experiences you can never experience. It is a passion."

"A passion!" He picked up a book that used to lie on the table. "To who?"

"To a lot. Me. It is a passion to me," she giggled as if there were something funny about it. Billy did not laugh. He was serious.

"And you can write?" he asked.

"Quite well," she added.

"My mother wrote well."

"What book do you have in your hands?" she was asking being curious. He handed the heavy book to her. "Ah," she gasped, "the Bible."

"Could you read this?" He handed her another object. Her head lifted and she saw it was a piece of paper with fine penmanship written on it. "My mother wrote it, I'm sure."

Abby's eyes sparkled in the sunlight as she looked up at Billy. "Yes, of course." Abby cleared her throat. "It is called *My Sunlight*. And yes, your mother wrote it." The paper read:

My sunlight comes in morning,
My sunlight leaves in the night.
My sunlight cannot burn out,
My sunlight will keep on shining.

My sunlight lives forever,
My sunlight can't fade away.
My sunlight is always true,
My sunlight is affection.

My sunlight keeps my soul live,
My sunlight lets me fly there.
My sunlight is my sunshine,
My sunlight is my family.

Abby rose her chin from the poem with a tear rolling down her cheek. "It's beautiful. So simple."

"That is what life was here, simple," he told her strongly. Billy was angry. He was much too strong to cry in front of her.

"There are so many books," Abby said, changing the subject.

"They're all my mother's and some of my father's. She read every single one of them." Silence overcame them. Billy was happy she was here. He was never able to read her poem. "Would you like to see upstairs?"

Abby nodded yes. She couldn't imagine the bedrooms. The house was all too beautiful. *Billy's mother must have been a wonderful woman,* she thought.

Billy and Abby climbed the grand staircase. There were two bedrooms upstairs.

"This was my parents' bedroom." Billy showed her to the larger of the two. A four-post bed centered the room. The bed was high. On each side, there were stools to climb up. The bedspread was a quilt with a floral of colors. Birds were sewn in and horses galloping away, along with coyotes howling in the moonlight and cows caring for their young.

The canopy that covered the bed was a purple silk. It was a beautiful bed and in the corner there was a vanity. It was wooden and a big mirror centered it. There was a hairbrush that was placed neatly on the surface. Cosmetics were all over the place and looked like her sister's dresser. Two tall dressers stood against two different walls and were full of fine clothing. An oil painting of the family of three was hung over the bed. His mother was beautiful and his father was handsome. Abby knew where Billy inherited his looks. He had his mother's eyes and his father's nose. He had his father's chin and his mother's full lips. On a wall, more books were stacked.

"More books?" she gasped.

"Her favorites," he said quickly.

The room was dark and abandoned. Everything was there like Billy's parents had left it the morning they died.

Billy left the room. Across the hallway was the door to his bedroom. He opened it and went inside. Abby followed him.

Billy's room was plain. A little wooden bed was against the wall. Another quilt was on his bed. It was blue with a little bit of red and yellow. Toys were everywhere. It was a boy's dream.

"Don't worry," he said, "I don't play with my toys."

Abby laughed. "That's good to know."

A bookshelf was on one of his walls. There were tall books, short books, and medium books.

"You have books in here too?" She walked over to the shelves. But Billy couldn't read!

"My mother used to read them to me," he whispered.

"Oh."

Billy exited his bedroom and went downstairs. "Would you like some water?" he asked politely. She took one last glance at his bedroom and went downstairs as well.

"Yes, please." She could not refuse. Gasping and awing all day made her thirsty. "I saw your garden outside." Abby leaned against the wall of the kitchen.

Billy poured water from a silver pitcher into a glass full of ice. "Yeah, it's a lot of work."

He handed her the glass of water. The water was refreshing. "I've always longed to have a garden."

"Well, you can help me with mine. I grow tomatoes, squash, beans, cucumbers and other vegetables too." Billy sipped his water from the glass he poured for himself.

"I've always wondered where you lived," Abby confessed.

"Why have you never asked?" he asked her.

"I don't know. I wish my house was like this, with so much love put into it."

"There isn't much. It's so lonely," he told her.

"What do you do after I leave?"

"Stay at the rock 'til late. It's very lonely."

"I can imagine," she agreed.

"Abby," he stuttered. He looked down at his glass, and then looked up. The deep blue of his eyes seemed to change into deep green in the sunshine.

"Yes?"

He was silent for a moment and wanted to say something, but the words wouldn't come out. "Never mind," Billy said to her.

"Can you believe how cold it is today?" she said changing the subject again.

"I noticed you're wearing a different dress."

"You're right." She grinned. "I figured my old dress was much

15

too dirty."

"It was," he agreed.

"What about you, you're dirty," she reminded him gently.

"Doesn't matter to me. It's not like anyone sees me."

"I do," she whispered. Abby ended the subject. She looked out the window and saw the sun setting. "Come on!" She grabbed Billy's hand and ran out the front door. Abby ran to the path with Billy running behind her. "We've got to see the sunset!"

When they both got to Old Mann Rock, they saw the last bit of sun for that day. The sun snuck behind the tall mountains like a child playing the game of hide-and-seek. It dragged colors of the rainbow down with its long yellow cape. The colors smothered the sky like an artist's painting would.

"Just in time," panted Abby. The sunset ended another perfect day at Old Mann Rock. "I must leave now."

"Yup."

They placed themselves into the canoe and Billy pushed off with his stick.

"Thank you for showing me your house."

"It wasn't much," he shrugged. "But I'm glad I've shared it with you."

"Yes, it is." She put her hand on his knee. "I like when you share things with me." They both smiled.

When they were approaching Abby's stop, they saw a shadowy figure on the bank. Was it someone looking for her? Had they found her secret hideaway?

Chapter 3

It was a man she had never seen before! He was fishing! Abby thought it was someone searching for her. Billy set the boat aside.

"Hello," the man said looking at Abby. He was surprised to see such a beautiful girl with a dirty boy.

"Hello," replied Abby.

"Hi," Billy said as though the man was suspicious.

Abby thought he was handsome. His eyes were a dark brown and his hair hid his forehead. He had clean clothes on and didn't seem like someone who fished very often.

"Doing some fishing?" Abby said trying to be friendly. They looked at each other.

"I am," he said weakly. "I am Nick Porter."

Abby held her hand out. "I am Abigail Cotter."

Nick took her hand and kissed it.

Abby blushed. "This is Billy," she introduced.

The men shook each other's hands. Billy didn't like Nick. He had something up his sleeve.

"Where are you going?" Nick asked.

"I'm just going home. Billy was kind enough to bring me." Abby climbed out of the canoe.

Nick looked at Billy. "Good man." Then he looked at Abby and winked at her.

"Better than some," Billy shrugged.

"Well, I can escort you home, if you'd like?" Nick was being a perfect gentleman.

"Of course." Abby took the offer with no regrets. "Good night, Billy." She looked one last look at his blue eyes for the night and smiled.

He smiled back, but he really wanted to frown. He was jealous. Not wanting to admit it, Billy stared at her figure until he could no longer see her. Why did he feel this way? It seemed that Abby always had a magic spell upon Billy like this. He had to be strong. Nick would not be on his list of favorite people. Billy decided to tell Abby tomorrow what he had wanted to tell her today.

Strolling through the woods at night was magical, Abby thought. "I am new in town," Nick said, starting a new conversation.

"Really? What brings you here?" she asked as if the town she lived in presently was nothing to live in.

"Actually, my father just moved here. I am visiting him from Harvard while he is ill."

"I'm so sorry about your father, but Harvard? You must be a smart man?"

His ego became larger than it was. A cocky grin came upon his face. "Maybe I am," he chuckled. "So is Billy your boyfriend?"

"No," she suspected the answer was what he wanted to hear. "Just a friend. A best friend actually."

"He has good manners," laughed Nick, sarcastically.

"Oh." She took Billy's side. "He's not used to being around people."

"Is he a fugitive?"

"No." Abby was insulted. She decided to give the conversation another try, so she would give him a second chance. "Do you like to read?"

"Yes, I do."

Abby smiled. "I love to read."

"Wow! Do you attend school?" he asked.

"No, my father said I didn't need to because I was dumb. But I know I am not."

"It is obvious you're not." They meandered through the woods a bit more, talking like old friends who haven't seen each other in a while.

They reached the Cotter General Store. "This is it," she said embarrassed.

"Your father owns that store?" he asked amazed.

"As you can see."

"Why, I was just in there today! I bought a few things for my father."

"Really? I don't stick around that much. In fact, I didn't stick around for dinner tonight."

"Oh, tell him you've been visiting a new friend who hopes to see you again." Nick grinned.

"Well, I don't think that will work, but I do hope to see you again." Abby tried to smile. "I wonder what I'm going to get tonight," she said under her breath.

"What did you say?" Nick missed her remark about her father.

"Oh, nothing," she said quickly. "Well, Good night, Mr. Porter."

"Oh, please, call me Nick," he insisted.

"Okay, Good night, Nick," she corrected.

"Good night, Abigail," he replied.

Abby turned toward the door that led to the store. She was about to turn around to tell him to call her Abby, but she felt she hadn't known him all too well yet. Although, on the first day she met Billy, she had insisted him to call her Abby. *Oh well*, she thought, *there will be other times.*

Her father stood inside. He had an angry expression on his face. This look always came before he whipped her. She knew what was coming. More pain, more fear. More thoughts on how she wished she hadn't come home that day. Why did she come home everyday? Why couldn't she just stay with Billy and have a peaceful life? Then she knew the answer. It was pride. She certainly didn't want to run away. What would people think of her? It was the fear Billy and others would think she was a coward for running away from her problems. How could she live like that?

"Abigail!" he exclaimed. "Where have you been all night?"

Abby took a few steps away from the door, so if Nick were still outside, he would have less of a chance of hearing. "I'm sorry. Nick Porter and I were talking."

"Well maybe Nick Porter should have some manners. It is very disrespectful of you to not show up for dinner."

She didn't have respect for him. She didn't want to be like him or her mother one bit. "What do you care?" she asked as she walked to the staircase.

"We had important people over."

"Important people? Oh, I forgot you don't care. I thought for maybe a second there, you were actually worried."

"What do you know?" Charles Cotter asked with a snarl expecting Abby not to say anything.

She decided to let it all out. She had nothing to lose. He was already going to whip her anyway. "I…I know that you don't love me," she stuttered trying to hold back the lonely tears.

"Well, who would?" he screamed.

She didn't stop. "I know you only love yourself!" She had to say no more. Sure enough, that long piece of leather was wrapped around his right hand. He had a tight grip, which made a fist. Abby swallowed hard and tried to prepare herself mentally for what was coming. It was no use. Every time he whipped her, it felt like new. She had always forgotten the horror.

The long whip, which seemed like a poisonous snake, came down on her back.

SMACK! SMACK! It was like the weapon was yelling.

"Don't ever disobey me again!" he screamed. He whipped Abby five more times. Blood was pouring from her body like water gushing in a wild waterfall.

Abby whimpered and fell to her knees. She hid her face with her hands.

She wanted it to STOP!

"Stop!" she pleaded.

He finally stopped.

Abby saw him lift the leather again and whip it down on her once more. This time, it came down on her left hip. She cried out. Now, she wanted Nick to hear her.

But he didn't. No one heard her. Her father kicked her, and then he left. She lay there crying and wishing she had never left Billy. It started raining. The rain was slapping against the glass of the windows. Thunder roared in the sky. Lightning lit the world up.

She didn't care about pride anymore. She would stay at Old Mann Rock tomorrow, and for the rest of her life.

She cried herself to sleep. She thought how wonderful life would be, helping Billy with the garden and perhaps teaching him how to read. That would be life.

Then she thought about his parents. *Who would murder such loving people and leave an innocent boy behind to live on his own? Who would have such a disturbed soul to ruin lives?* Abby certainly did not know the answer. Whoever it was, she hoped would be punished.

The next morning, Abby found herself on the floor of the store. Puddles of blood marked where she slept. Her back ached. Her hip ached. Her whole body ached. She lifted herself to her feet and went to her bedroom.

Abby took off her bloodstained dress and put on a clean one. She twirled because the skirt was big, in the shape of a teacup. Then she stopped. Her cuts were burning. Abby brushed her long black hair until all of the snarls were gone.

She headed downstairs.

Breakfast was the same as yesterday. Her father said nothing. Her younger sister's yellow curls bounced up and down, her blue eyes peering at her father once in a while. Her older sister Hattie's long, straight blonde hair was fashionably in a tight bun today. Hattie didn't look at anyone. She concentrated on her food.

Abby's sisters were both pudgy. They both had round faces with freckles dotted here and there. Abby looked very different than them. Her black hair and eyes certainly did not match their blonde hair and blue eyes. Abby's face was not round and she wasn't pudgy.

Charles ascended from his chair and left.

Abby wasted no time helping her mother with the dishes; after all she was not coming back.

Abby went through the front door with not a look back. I will not regret this, she promised to herself. She ran through the woods to get

21

to the river, and the cool air blew against her face with her long hair dangling in thin air. She loved these cool days. With some of the birds migrating south, the forest was quieter.

When she approached the river, Billy wasn't there. Then she saw him down the river coming. "I beat you," she bragged as he reached the bank.

"For once," he reminded. "Why are you so early?"

"I have some good news."

Billy looked down. "Me first. Please?" He looked up at her for a while. Her smile faded from his look.

"Okay," she said worried. He was sad, she knew.

Billy helped her in. He sat down after her and slowly pushed off with his long pole.

"Billy, what's the matter?" she asked, not wanting to know the answer, for she knew it wasn't good news.

"Yesterday," he said dragging his answer, "I wanted to tell you something."

"Oh, I remember," she said to Billy restoring the beautiful day.

"Well, I want to tell you today."

"Okay."

"I...I," he stuttered.

"What?"

"I have to leave," he told her finally getting the answer out.

"Where are you going?" Abby asked with a smile appearing, knowing he was going for a few months.

"No, I'm leaving Old Mann Rock. Forever. I won't be back," he cleared up.

"What?" She was shocked. "Why?"

"To get out of danger."

"You're running away!" she screamed. "Here yesterday, I was debating if I should live at Old Mann Rock."

"You were going to live here? You can't. You need your family. They love you."

"No they don't!" Abby burst into tears.

"What's wrong?" There was a secret, he knew. A secret she never told him.

"Here," she said crying, "unbutton my dress." Abby turned her back to him, so he could.

As he started unbuttoning, he saw fresh cuts with blood still dribbling out. "Who did this to you?" he demanded Abby to answer. "Was it Nick?"

"No!" she yelled. "It was my father!" She turned and looked at him.

"How long has this been going on, Abby?" He was furious. Why would someone do that to her?

Her eyes were swelled up from crying. "Why do you have to leave?"

"I don't. The people who killed my parents told me they would be back."

"For you?" she gasped.

"Yeah. I want to put you out of danger, too. That's why you can't come back to Old Mann Rock again."

"But…"

"Promise?" he begged.

"No," she couldn't promise something as hard as this.

"Abby!" he yelled. "You are so difficult!"

"No! I can't!" Abby started to cry even more.

They came to Old Mann Rock. They climbed the rock together for the last time.

Billy faced Abby and wiped away a tear with his rough thumb. "Abby, please stop crying."

"You don't understand. You're the only person I care about, Billy." She buried her restless head in her knees.

Billy put his hand on her shoulder like he did the first day they met. "I want to tell you, I'll leave a boat for you. So you can come here Christmas day. Your present will be waiting."

"Where would you get a boat?" she asked a little skeptical as she rose her head from her lap.

"We have an old one," he told her. "I'm taking a left on the fork in the river."

"You don't know where you're going. It could be dangerous."

"I'll be fine. Don't you worry your pretty little head off because of me," he reassured her.

A smile slowly came upon her face. "You think I'm pretty?" she was amazed.

"No one's ever told you?"

"No," she shrugged.

"I do. I think you're beautiful, Abby." He took a piece of her long, silky hair and fiddled it between his fingers.

Abby looked at his eyes. They weren't a mystery anymore. The mystery was how he looked at her. He thought she was beautiful! His eyes studied her hair. He seemed to play with it as if he were a kitten fooling around with a piece of yarn.

Billy looked up at her and caught her looking at him funny. "Let's go get that boat."

"Yeah," she said. Her stare had been broken.

Billy stood up and then helped Abby to her feet. "So, is Nick your boyfriend now?" Had she put a magical spell on someone else?

Abby scrunched up her nose. "No. He's nice, but he's too..." She searched for the right words. "I don't know. I can't explain it."

They went to the path and entered. The woods were beautiful. Yesterday, Abby was so curious with the surprise, she didn't even bother to look at the nature. This forest was much more elegant than the one she walked through everyday. Every tree that turned to colors was remarkable. Could it be they were all enchanted?

They reached Billy's home. "The boat is out back," Billy said as he broke the barrier of Abby's concentration.

Abby followed him in back of the house. An older canoe was turned upside down against the logs.

"It's old, I know," he confessed.

"It will do just fine." Her eyes smiled.

"Would you help me carry it to the rock?" he asked politely.

She nodded. Abby walked over to it, as well as Billy. They lifted it over their shoulders and were well on their way.

"Do you have everything packed? At least, what you need?" she asked in concern as they carried the boat through the woods.

"Would you stop worrying?"

"Do you?" She stopped in her tracks.

"I do."

She started moving again. The boat was heavy on both of their shoulders. Although, it was a cold day, they both started to perspire.

When they ended their haul, they plopped the boat in the river.

"Your new boat," he told her.

"But I don't want a new boat, Billy. I need you." One of the thousand tears she would shed that day ran down her red cheek.

He turned away from her. "Please, Abby, don't make it worse…"

She couldn't help but intrude. "Make it worse than it already is? My God, I don't know if I'll ever see you again!"

Billy turned to face her. "I hope that's not true," he told her.

Abby wrapped her arms around him. He did the same. She buried her head in his neck. He felt her tears dribble onto his skin.

The warmth of Abby's body came onto his bare skin. She let go of him. "Promise me, you'll be careful?" she sniffled.

"Promise," he whispered gently.

"Maybe I should go?" she suggested.

"Nah," he told her, "It's not even near sunset. But you must promise me something."

"No, Billy, I can't promise that."

He put his hand on her cold cheek and wiped away another tear. "No, not that. Promise me you'll try to be good for your father. So he won't hurt you anymore?"

"I'll try," she bargained.

"Promise me?" he pleaded.

"All right, I promise."

"Come on," he said. He led her to the rock.

"One last time." She tried to smile.

"Your Christmas present," he mentioned once again. "It's in my parent's bedroom. You'll be able to see it when you open the door. But you must promise me again. Promise you won't go in there until Christmas?"

"I promise," she agreed.

"Oh." He took a small object out of his pocket. "Your other gift." He handed her a heart on a chain. She took it with great care. "It was my mother's."

"I can't take this," she told him in awe. It was beautiful. The heart was a locket with two little diamonds on the cover. She opened it and saw his mother and father in one picture on one side, and Billy in another picture on the other side.

"She wanted you to have it actually," he assured her. "She said, 'Give it to your best girl.' And you're my best girl."

"Thank you so much." *How beautiful,* she thought. "Would you put it on for me?" she asked kindly. She turned around and handed Billy the necklace. When he was finished, she turned to face him. "I must go now," she decided. Another tear was made. "I promise to be careful of my father," she chuckled.

Billy smiled. "Okay."

"To make it easier, would it be all right if I went alone?" she asked trying not to be too forward.

"Fine," he agreed.

As more pearls rode her face, she would wish he didn't have to leave. "Goodbye, Billy."

"Goodbye, Abby," he said, trying to be strong.

Abby leaned to Billy and kissed him on his cheek. "Bye," she whispered as he turned away.

He caught her arm just before she left. She turned around and looked in his eyes once more and was swept away. This time, he leaned into her and pressed his mouth to her lips. A long kiss took place and a feeling burst inside both of them. They didn't want to leave. They feared they would never see each other's face again. Abby put both of her hands on his cheeks and pressed her lips to his once more.

"Please don't leave me," she said when she caught her breath.

"It's not for me, it's for you," he whispered as he glared in her eyes. He knew her spell would never fade.

Abby wiped away her tears and turned to board the old canoe.

Billy followed. "Here, you can keep my stick."

"Thank you so much. For everything." She pushed off the bank with Billy's stick. When she passed the rock, she looked back. Billy stood on the rock and watched her leave. The sun was setting and purple, red, and blue was in the background. His hair blew in the breeze. She turned and burst into tears.

Why would God put us on Earth and have us meet, if we only had to part? she thought. Abby had the urge to jump out of the boat and swim back to him, but she didn't want to make it worst.

Billy sat down on the rock and stared at her, until he couldn't see her anymore. A tear ran down his face. He kept it in, to be strong for her, but he couldn't be strong anymore. He already missed her so much.

Already.

This magic spell, which Abby had put on him, was it love?

Chapter 4

Billy stretched his long arms out as he pulled himself out of bed.

He had been dreaming; the dream was so real. A dream about Abby always felt real.

Why?

He missed her more. He didn't want to leave at all, but he had to. There was no choice to it. A sacrifice was being made, he knew.

Abby taught him so much. She taught him everything he knew from the long talks, which took place during the cool days. He loved those days as well as the summer days. Old Mann Rock was like heaven had touched down on Earth. Was that possible?

He put his pair of clean pants on, combed his fingers through his hair, and grabbed his gold pocket watch from the surface of his bureau.

The pocket watch had been his father's. Billy had unclipped it from the inside of his jacket when he found him dead. He could remember the day like it was yesterday.

1869

Billy woke up to a gunshot in the middle of the night. Although he was nine, he knew something was wrong. He had heard his parents talking about trouble with other people before and it made him worried.

He bolted out of bed and ran downstairs. "Mom!" he cried. "Dad!" *Where are they?* he thought frantically. "Anyone here?" He looked all around the house and found the back door wide open. He sprinted out. "Mom! Dad! Where are you?" His eyes filled with water.

As he searched with his eyes through the woods, he saw a dim light at Old Mann Rock. Billy ran to the path. As he came closer, he slowed down. There were people there. The only thing he could make out were people, dragging something on the rock.

"We'll be back," one man said, "for the kid next time." The man had a deep scratchy voice and then he put his arm around a woman. "Let's go," he told her. Two other men followed the couple into their boat and they pushed off the bank.

"Are my parents laying on the rock?" he asked God praying the answer was no. Billy crept up on the rock and saw his parents lifeless and blood seeping out of them onto the rock.

"Billy." He heard his mother's soft voice. "Come here, my son," she said in pain.

He hated when she was in pain along with his father. "Mama," he whispered. Billy laid himself in between his mother and father. "Is Daddy..." he couldn't finish the question.

"Oh, my dear, I believe so," she told him with her lips trembling. "Billy, take his watch." Billy obeyed and unclipped his father's watch. "And take this," she pleaded as she pointed to her locket which hung around her neck. "Give it to your best girl." She swallowed hard.

"Okay, Mama," he assured her.

"I love you, my baby," she said. "I will always be with you and so will your father."

Billy glanced at his father, whose eyes were still open. Billy shut them with his fingers shaking with horror.

"Goodbye, Billy," his mother whispered and shut her own eyes.

"Mama! Mama!" he screamed. Billy sat up and saw the dim light turn the corner of the river. "Mama! Wake up!" Billy couldn't lose her! He was only nine! "Mama!" he cried. "Wake up! Please wake up!" He shook her to wake her, but she lay there without a flinch. Then he shook his father. "Daddy! Wake up! No God! Please don't! No!" He couldn't bare it. He lay back down and cried himself to sleep.

Next morning, he woke up at dawn still remembering the horror. Billy rose to his feet and looked down at the two bodies he slept between. He turned around and saw the sunrise quickly. It was as if the sun was shouting, "Billy, you'll be okay. Everything will be okay soon." But Billy knew that was not possible. Someone had been so cruel to kill them. He needed his parents.

The water splashed as he jumped from the rock to rinse off the drying blood of his parents. Billy walked on shore rubbing his face with his hands. He peered at his parents and wished they were still alive.

Billy took the shovel, which had a place in the shed. He dug a ditch in back of the rock, to be sure they lay near the rock, where he hoped would be his home forever. He dragged his father first, trying to make sure not to twist him around. His father's head bobbed over the rocks, as Billy tried to pull the heavy body to his grave. His mother was much lighter, but before he placed her in the homemade grave, he unlatched her necklace and put it in his pocket.

His best girl? He definitely never wanted to like girls. *But maybe I will have a best girl one day,* he thought.

Billy took one last glance at the two mangled figures covered in dirt, and started filling the hole in.

He looked all around for some kind of object to mark their grace. Billy found a small American flag upstairs, which his father loved. He fought in the war, when Billy was only one. Every night, his mother would rock him in the rocking chair reading him the Bible and then she would tell him, "Your father's coming home soon, my baby, just you wait."

And he did. With nothing but dirt and a few bruises on him, he came home to his loving family. That's why he loved that flag.

Billy dug the stick into the soil and watched as it waved freely, marking where his parents lay. He picked two flowers from the ground and neatly placed them at the bottom of the stick to show two people lay there dead. One for each of them.

1877

Billy climbed himself out of his gaze. He proceeded to place the watch in his pocket and looked around his bedroom.

Was he forgetting something?

His quilt. Billy needed it because he knew winter was coming. He bundled up the blanket in a big ball and left the room.

In the hallway, he placed the bedspread on the floor and went into his parents' bedroom. He wanted to make sure Abby's gift was still perfect like he left it yesterday. It hadn't moved. He was sure of that.

Billy looked around his mother and father's bedroom and took a deep breath. He watched as the lace draped over the four posts. It was a lovely room. The big windows trimmed with more lace, which almost fell off the windowsill from the many years it remained there untouched.

Billy remembered the mornings when his parents were still alive. His father would always be up and working on something new around the house. His mother would be still in bed sleeping softly like a queen alone in the big bed. Billy would wake up before her and sneak into her bed. He'd lay his gentle head upon her stomach and sleep a little longer.

When she would wake, she usually placed his head on the pillow carefully. She'd sit at her vanity and comb her long hair and hum to herself softly. Billy always woke up from her singing.

"Good morning, Mama," he would say drowsily.

"Good morning, my baby," she'd reply. She always called him her baby. Billy didn't like it very much, but he tolerated it.

Now he longed to hear her say, "Good morning, my baby," one more time. But he couldn't. He could never hear her say it again because she was gone. Gone forever.

He went to his mother's vanity where there was money hidden. He pulled it all out. There was a lot and he would need it to start his new life.

Billy walked to the doorway, picked up his quilt and headed for downstairs. He ate the last bit of fish left from dinner for breakfast and decided to leave. He wouldn't wait to see if Abby would come around because the idea was stupid. *No*, he thought, *I'm going to leave now. Today. This minute.* He took the gas lantern, which hung over the table. The nights will be best to travel. There was less chance of getting into trouble.

He slipped on his heavy boots and tied their laces tight. When he wore his boots, they made him walk louder. He could remember the day his father came home from the war, wearing the same boots.

Billy sighed. He walked to the front door loudly and turned around to leave. Standing before his house, was a figure. His vision blurred, for he thought it was Abby. He turned and looked in his house. He was confused.

"Hello," she said a little fearful.

"Hi," he said to the stranger after he turned again to face the girl. She started up the steps.

"Could you help me?" she asked quietly.

"Um…" Billy didn't know what to say. "What can I do for you?" He looked down at her round stomach, and then looked at her face. Billy knew this pregnant girl was only about fifteen.

"I need help."

"What kind of help?" he asked calmly.

Last night's whipping was harsh, Abby thought as she walked through the woods. The leaves were falling off their limbs now. They seemed to be sad. They appeared to share her pain. Yesterday when she went home, her father was furious. That time, her mother joined in with his pleasure.

"You little brat!" her mother screamed as she lifted the weapon over Abby's bloody back. They hurt her because Abby had not helped her with the dishes that morning. The pain was overbearing. But Abby let it all go and took a deep breath.

She climbed a tree near the river where its branches hung over the water. Just in case Billy decided to come by.

Abby laid her sore back against the large trunk and opened a book. The book had blank pages in it. There she would write as often as she could. Since Billy wouldn't be around to talk to, she'd write her thoughts down instead. She wrote on the first page:

September 18, 1877

Today I start you, dear diary. Billy, my best friend has long gone for an adventure. So I must write my ideas instead. My name is Abigail Caroline Cotter. I like to be called Abby, though. Cotter is my horrid last name for which I don't care for. My parents are awful people. They beat me when I do one small mistake. Oh well, that is my life. I have two sisters; Hattie and Constance. Constance is nice, but Hattie is a cow, if you ask me. When Hattie's hair pokes, she never is punished. My one wish would to have different parents. Sometimes, I wonder why I look so different. Is it because I was supposed to be like this or is it because I do have other parents somewhere out there? Oh, I must go. I do believe I see a boat rowing down the river. Could it be Billy?

Yours truly,
Abby

Abby closed her diary so fast; it almost fell to the ground. As the object came closer, she saw it wasn't Billy. It was two young men floating down river. Once in a while, she and Billy would see them row down. They'd wave and say their hellos and keep going.

The men were making complete fools of themselves. Abby considered the thought they weren't just idiots, but drunks.

Abby could not be seen from where they were. She giggled and it turned to a laugh. She put her hand over her mouth to stop the sound. They rocked the small boat back and forth and nearly tipped over.

"La...la...la...la...!" one man sang his heart out holding a bottle in his hand. He was singing to the world.

"So...so...so...so...!" the other drunk replied in a deeper voice. Then the boat was rocking so hard, it flipped over. They went underwater and one came up to say: "So...so..."

"La...la...la..."

"So!" he finished the song. They climbed back into the white rowboat and continued drifting down the body of water.

Abby sighed. She was so bored. Suddenly, she knew what she'd do. *I'm going to see if Billy is still there*, she thought as she jumped down to Earth.

She was delaying his voyage. He needed to go. She was about five months pregnant and Billy couldn't just leave her out there. The girl's name was Christina. She was in pain.

Why would she be in pain? He did know about babies and how they were made, but he didn't understand why she was in pain. Billy gave her a hot towel and a bucket of steaming water to put her feet in.

"Thank you so much, Billy," she said gratefully. "I appreciate it."

"Ah, it was nothing," he assured her as he sat down across from her.

"Nice house. It is yours, isn't it?" she said admiring it, but not as much as Abby did the day before.

"Thanks, it…"

"Oh…!" she groaned as she held her stomach.

"What's wrong?" Billy panicked.

"Oh," she smiled, obviously becoming relieved. "It's only the baby kicking."

"Oh."

"Come here," she patted the empty seat next to her. "Come and feel it."

"Okay." Billy went to sit down next to her.

"Here," she said as she took his two fingers and placed them on the spot where the baby was fussy. Billy felt movement. He was amazed!

"Wow!" He was like a child when their eyes would light up on Christmas morning.

"Billy," she said cunning, "I wish you were the father."

Billy's eyes became larger than they already were. *What was this girl thinking?* He said nothing.

"Kiss me, you fool!" she yelled deliriously. Christina cupped his cheeks with her hands and forced his head to hers.

That was uncalled for, Billy thought. "No wonder you're pregnant!" he yelled, not able to keep it in any longer. Then he heard the front door close shut.

Abby approached the familiar spot on the river. She climbed the rock and saw Billy's boat still there. She thought he would be at the rock waiting for her just as he saw her leave. *He must be at his house,* she thought. Abby walked to the path and hiked the short distance not wanting to wait to see his beautiful face again.

She climbed the noisy steps, not trying to make a sound. She wanted to surprise him. Abby opened the door and saw the most horrible sight, which gave her the worst feeling. Her eyes filled up with water and began to run down her face. She stood there shocked. Then she saw Billy looking at her.

"Abby!" he yelled. He bolted from the loveseat like a dart shooting for the board. "Wait! Please! No!" His voice filled with pain.

Abby ran away. She ran all the way to her boat and tried quickly to untie the rope from the tree. He was gaining on her.

"Abby!" he shouted. "Wait! I can explain!" He saw her get into the boat. He ran to the rock and watched her leave.

"There's no need for explaining," she replied sobbing. "You've already done it all!"

"But..."

"No, forget it. Forget everything! Never come back!" She stormed through the water with her stick.

Billy dove into the water and swam hard to her. She fought. She didn't want him to be there. She wanted to get away. The boat flipped and Abby rose to the top of the water.

"I hope you don't mean that," he whispered.

She was drenched and cold. "I do," she sniffled. "Never come back. I can't tell you how I felt just now."

"She kissed me!" he exclaimed.

"And you pushed away?" She waited for his reply and shook her head slowly. "I didn't think so."

"But, Abby, I felt nothing."

"I have to go," she said stubbornly and pushed away. "I should have never come." Abby rolled the old boat over and lifted herself back in.

"Misery! Why do I put myself in misery?" she asked herself. She couldn't figure out the answer. The nerve of him! This time, she didn't look back for she thought she would jump back in and forgive him. No! No! She was so stubborn and almost mean. But, was he telling her the truth?

Abby didn't want to think anymore. She would go home...and do what? There was nothing to do. She would go into town. *Maybe I can find some trouble*, she thought. She didn't care anymore.

Billy didn't know what to do. He didn't know what would happen. Why did he have to leave like this? Why? It was just a bad ending. But endings were supposed to be good.

"Billy!" Christina shouted from the rock. "Are you okay, sweetie?"

Sweetie! Billy swam to shore, then lifted himself on the rock and stood by Christina. "First of all, I am not your sweetie."

"Yes you are," she told him swiping her hand across his chest. "You kissed me."

"And second of all, I didn't kiss you. You kissed me."

"Didn't you like it?" she asked stretching her grin wider.

Billy sighed. "No, I didn't." Christina's grin turned to a frown.

"Was that your girlfriend? Is that why she was mad?"

"No, she's not."

"Is Abby your friend?" Christina asked.

"Yeah, she is...How did you know her name?" Billy was startled.

"Everyone knows her. Everyone wonders where she disappears to. I heard my brother likes her."

"Who's your brother?" Billy was jealous.

"Nick."

"Nick Porter?" Billy was furious.

"Why, yes. Do you know him?"

Billy was trying to stay cool. "I've heard of him," he shrugged.

"I hear her father's a real jerk."

"Yeah, he is to her," Billy agreed.

"Well, that's enough talk about her," Christina said slyly. "Let's talk about you on the couch."

"No!" Billy was insulted. "You're pregnant."

"But, Billy, you're so handsome." Christina ran her fingers through his hair. "You're so strong and handsome."

"You already said that." That woman was crazy.

"Oops! Will you forgive me?"

"The point is, Christina, I was supposed to leave today."

"I'll go with you!" she said, excited.

"No! No! You can't. I'll take you back from wherever you came and then I'm leaving."

"But, Billy, can't you be delayed?" she asked, whining.

"No! Abby!" he yelled.

Christina looked up at Billy with her big eyes and saw pain overcome his face. "Wrong girl."

"Sorry," he apologized. "I must go. Get in the boat."

"All right! All right!" Christina went to the boat and climbed in.

"Hold on. I have to make sure of something."

Billy ran into the woods and paced to the tall building, which stood all alone. The door wasn't closed. Billy shut it. He tidied up the house for Abby when she would come back. If she ever came back. Billy raced back to the boat and just wanted to leave, finally.

"I'll bring you to the main port," Billy told the pregnant girl as he rowed the tiny boat.

"You know, Billy, you're a real gentleman." Christina smiled. "If you were my brother and if I were Abby, you would have taken advantage of me. But you wouldn't." She shook her head.

"What do you know about Abby's father?" Billy asked curious.

"Not much. He's a con artist, who always gets out of jail." Christina giggled.

Billy didn't find it amusing. "What's so funny about it?"

"They *both* deserve it. Her and her husband. She deserves to be in jail as much as her pig of a husband."

The fork of the river was ahead. Billy steered the canoe left. He would start his journey at the harbor. Billy hasn't seen the harbor in years. He used to come here once in a while when his mother needed supplies. The waterfront was so crowded. Billy could see it as he exited the tributary onto the Connecticut River. There were men working, ships sailing in and out to deliver their finest treasures.

Billy's plan was to drift down the main river down to Connecticut. He knew after Connecticut was the ocean and a canoe couldn't survive in such a big, New World.

"Right here's fine, thank you," Christina insisted. Billy helped her out safely.

"Would you like me to bring you home?"

"No," she said, "I'm fine."

"Are there any bakeries or anything 'round here, like stores?" Billy asked before she turned to leave.

"Well, Abby's folks' store is around the corner. But other than that, there's a small restaurant about a quarter of a mile on Main Street."

"Oh yeah, I remember that. Thanks, Christina." She turned to leave. "Oh, good luck with your baby."

"Thanks, Billy." Christina kept walking.

"Yup." Billy walked on shore, took the rope and tied it around a tree so it wouldn't drift off. Billy watched as men and boys loaded and unloaded boxes off and on the ships.

"Billy?" A boy about Billy's age apparently recognized him. "Billy, is that you?" Billy turned around to see the man calling him. "It's me, buddy."

Billy stared at the familiar face. "Jack? Is that you?" Billy's eyes were almost as wide as two silver dollars. The two childhood friends hugged each other and added a hard, friendly pat to each other's backs. "My God, Jack, it's been so long."

"I know. I always wondered what happened to you."

"Long story. I'm hungry. Want a bite to eat? My treat."

"Sure," Jack said.

Billy laughed. "What happened to you?"

Jack was soaked. "Some girl pushed me into the water."

"That's Jack, always friendly with the ladies."

"You know it."

The friends walked onto Main Street talking about what had been going on. Billy looked around and thought how different it looked. It seemed renovated. With the town being a major port on the river, things needed to be new. There were little children scurrying in the streets playing games while their mothers and fathers made a living at various trades.

"Everything has changed, Jack. It's so different from when we were kids."

"Sure is," Jack agreed.

"It's still here," Billy pointed to the old restaurant they were about to enter.

"Yeah, old, but still serving good food." Jack opened the door and went in. Billy followed. They both sat near the window and immediately knew what they would order.

Then Billy saw Abby walking in the street next with his worse nightmare, Nick Porter. Billy stared at her and ignored Jack.

"Billy? Billy?" Jack broke Billy's concentration.

"Looking at Abigail Cotter? Most guys like to."

"Yeah."

"Gorgeous, isn't she?"

"Yeah," Billy agreed. "She is. Abby is beautiful."

"Ya' know her?" Jack asked Billy confused.

"I do. I got to tell you a whole lot, Jack."

"What?"

Billy told him about how his parents died as they ate their ordered stew. Neither Jack, nor anyone else in the town knew they were dead. Billy told Jack about Old Mann Rock and Abby. He explained why he had to leave.

"Take care of her, Jack," Billy demanded.

"I will," Jack said in a promising tone.

"She means a lot to me, and Nick Porter won't get in the way of it."

"But, Billy, you're running away."

"I know! I know! I have nothing else to do! If I stay here they will come after me and I don't want her being with me when they do come back. My life was too good to be true."

"Yeah, it was. Why wouldn't you let her go with you, Billy?"

"I don't know. I'm so confused." Billy sighed.

"Well I say, Billy, you're in love with Abby."

"Ya' think? My God, I haven't only been thinking about that since we kissed each other."

"I would be too. Well, I really can't help you there, Billy."

"Hey, come with me."

"What?"

"Jack, come with me down river."

"Sorry, Billy, but even you couldn't leave if you were me. I have a good job and my mom's real sick."

"Sorry about that," Billy said apologetic.

"No problem, but I wish you the best of luck, my friend."

"Thanks. Here's some money. Could you leave the amount that it says on the bill?"

"Sure," Jack said willingly knowing Billy was not educated. He laid the amount of money on the table along with a small tip and the friends went out the door.

"Well, I have to get going now," Billy said saying another hard goodbye.

"Yeah." Jack looked down and kicked the dirt with his leather boot. "Have a good trip and I'll take care of Abby. Thanks for lunch."

"Yeah, bye, Jack."

"Bye, Billy. Be safe. Don't be too crazy now."

"I won't." The friends hugged each other like they had when they said hello, but this time it was goodbye.

Billy walked away toward the river being aware Abby could be around. But he didn't see her, nor hear her.

He untied the rope around the tree and rowed out to the wide river. He knew that was his last chance to be with Abby, but he kept going. He was eager to make it to his destination, Connecticut. He didn't know how long it would take; he had no idea what lay ahead.

Chapter 5

September 18, 1877

*How could Billy do that to me? How could he kiss
Christina Porter? She's such an…I don't know. I hope she
doesn't know the father of her baby. How could I be so mean?
I'm mad at Billy, not Christina. I do hope Billy is long gone
by now. I hope he never comes back. Well, no I don't. I don't
know what I want. But I do know I want to be crazy tonight.*

Yours truly,
Abby

Abby climbed out of the old, beat-up canoe and picked up her
soaking wet diary out of it. She saved it right before she flipped
over. She was about to hit Billy with it in the head, but instead, she
tipped over. Abby, wet and cold, stormed through the forest paying
no attention to the trees.

"Hey, Abby," Nick greeted her as she approached him.

Abby smiled. "Hello, Nick."

"Listen, I was wondering if you would like to go to a party with
me tonight? As my date?"

"Um…" Abby bit her lip. "Sure, I'd love to."

"Okay then, pick you up at eight?"

"Sure," she agreed. "Nick?"

"Yes, beautiful?"

Abby blushed. "Would you like to see the sunset at the waterfront.
If we go now, we'll make it."

"Yeah, I'd love to." They walked on Main Street to the harbor.
"Come on," Nick said as he took her hand. "We can go on one of
these ships. They won't leave now. They're docked for the night."

41

They snuck on a cargo ship, leaned against the bow of the big boat, and watched the sun go to sleep for the night.   "It's beautiful," Abby admired.

"Yes it is. Did you know…?" Nick went on and on, but Abby couldn't hear him anymore. She saw Billy drifting in his little canoe down the huge river. She ached for him. *Be careful,* she thought.

"Be careful," she said out loud.

"Huh?" Nick asked, confused.

"Never mind," she shrugged. "Keep going."

"Well as I was saying…." He went on again.

Billy, if you can hear me, Abby thought. She suddenly remembered the disgusting kiss today. "I hate you!" she screamed out loud.

"What?" Nick was baffled.

"Sorry, Nick, I was thinking of something else."

"Oh, well as I was…" Nick was interrupted again, but not by Abby.

"Hey!" a man said with a thunderous voice. "You're not supposed to be up here. Get off now, or I'll have you both arrested!" He was irritated.

"Damn!" Nick said.

"Come on," Abby took Nick's hand and jumped over the side of the boat. Nick jumped in after her.

"Good thinking," Nick praised her after they both came up to breathe.

"Thanks," she said looking up at the old man peering down at them. "But I think we should get out of here."

Abby went upstairs to her bedroom and put on a dry dress. But this time, her party dress. She wanted to look good for Nick. Abby combed her long hair with her hairbrush and went into a sudden daze.

What if Billy got hurt?

Abby shook her head, No! She was mad at him. She wouldn't think about him. She would concentrate on her appearance. Her sisters weren't home! What could she use?

Abby snuck into Hattie's bedroom and sat at her vanity, feeling important. She put on the pinkest blush and the reddest lipstick. Her lips looked like flames burning in the night sky.

Hattie's diamonds! Abby went into her jewelry box and picked out two diamond earrings and one sparkling necklace. She put them on for she thought she was beautiful!

"My dress! This won't do!" She went to Hattie's trunk and pulled out a red dress with black lace. It fit her perfectly. Then she slipped on the elbow-high lace gloves. She was ready to appear beautiful in front of the rest of the town. Dinner was not an issue in her house tonight. Her parents knew she was going to the party.

With her hair wild as night, she crept downstairs. *Good*, she thought, *no one's in the kitchen.*

As she slipped out the back door, she held her cloak in her arms as a cover up for when she came back. She was to be home by eleven o'clock, even though no one cared.

Abby looked at the full moon. The trees rattled from the cool breeze soaring through them. She walked to the river, where Nick would meet her. She walked slowly and admired, once again, the forest at night. She loved it. Abby smiled under the moon and reached the roaring river. Nick wasn't there yet.

Abby sat in the canoe and waited for him. She put her hand in the water and felt the cool, clear river run through her fingers.

"Look at you."

Abby jumped. She was startled. "What?"

"You look more beautiful than ever. If that's possible," Nick raved.

"Thank you," she blushed.

"Are you ready, sweetheart?"

Sweetheart! Abby was puzzled, but she could get used to this. She grinned. "Yes, I am."

Nick took her arm around his. "Great, let's go."

"Yes, let's," Abby had a nervous, but excited tone in her voice. They started to walk.

"Are you nervous?" Nick guessed her feelings.

She nodded. "I am. Are you?" she confessed.

"Sort of. After all, the party is for me."

"It is?" Abby was embarrassed. "I had no idea it was for you!"

"Yes it is. They're holding it for me because I'm leaving soon."

"Oh no. When?"

"I'm not sure, but I must go back to school. The year already started. I need to get back to my studies."

"But your father…"

Nick interrupted. "Well, unless he becomes more ill than he already is, I'm leaving."

"Well, I wish your father would get better, but I do wish you'd stay."

"Me too. I like you a lot."

Abby didn't know what to say. "So do I," she lied.

As they approached the outdoor party at the harbor, Abby began experiencing butterflies in her stomach. She felt them when she kissed…No! Stop thinking about him!

People were everywhere. Abby didn't know a lot of them but they appeared to know her. Sometimes, in town, people would come up to her and ask where she'd been lately. Why she was never around. She would shake her head and say, "I haven't seen you in a while, either."

Abby looked at the other women there. She was certainly in style. Hattie never wore that particular because she was too fat. One of their cousins from London had sent her the dress as a gift, unaware of how many pounds she gained.

"You look better than the rest of the women here," Nick whispered to her.

"Thank you," Abby smiled. Nick placed his hand on her back, leading the way. "Lovely party."

"I agree. But they didn't have to do it for me."

"Well, I don't see why not. You're a great man, Nick."

"Well, if I don't say so myself," Nick replied, boastful as ever.

Then, Abby's not-so favorite person showed up. "Well hello, Nick. Hello, Abby."

"Hello, Christina," Nick replied with one nod.

"Hi, Christina," Abby tried to smile. "I'm going to get something to drink. Would you like me to get you something?"

"No thanks, darling," Nick said. Abby walked away.

"Well, it looks as though Abby Cotter has you wrapped around her finger."

"Yeah," Nick sighed gazing at Abby.

"I was talking to one of her friends, Billy."

"Oh, I know him," Nick said sounding agitated.

"Well, he's going down the Connecticut River as we speak. He's not coming back, either."

"Are you serious?" Nick's eyes lit up.

"It's true, big brother."

Abby walked over to the bar. "Could I have some water please?" she asked the man standing behind the counter.

"Well, well, well, Abby Cotter. You look beautiful tonight."

Abby turned for she knew whom it was. "Jack, please, leave me alone."

"That's not very lady-like, Abby. But I must say with a little touch of lipstick, you resemble a doll."

"Thank you," she said, trying to sound polite.

"Here's your water, ma'am," the bartender said as he handed Abby the glass of clear water.

Abby sipped the cold beverage. "Thank you."

"I hear you're present with Nick, the guest of honor," Jack said trying to make conversation.

"Yes, I am." Abby disliked Jack very much. He was rude and obnoxious. Of course, she only thought that because he pulled her hair when they were younger for no reason.

"But, Billy wouldn't like it."

Abby was about to walk away, but when she heard his name, her eyes grew large. She almost choked on the water she was drinking. "You know Billy?"

"Saw him today. Here actually. But he left."

"I know."

45

"Listen to me, Abby. Stay away from Nick. He's not good. He'll take advantage of you."

"How insulting!" She had heard enough of this. Abby walked away.

"Wait!"

"What?" She turned around.

"Believe me."

"No, I won't! You're a fool, Jack, and you'll always be one!" her voice became louder. "So leave me alone and let me take care of myself. I'm a big girl now."

Jack scanned her with his eyes, being obvious. "Well, I can see that!"

"Jack!"

"Sorry! Abby, I say you're the fool not to believe me!"

Abby was outraged. "Well, we all have our opinions, don't we?"

The party became silent. Everyone was staring at the two of them arguing.

"Is this man bothering you, Abby?" Nick asked, stepping in.

"This is none of your business, Porter," Jack snapped.

"Yes he is, Nick," Abby told him.

"Could someone get him out of here?" Nick demanded. Two large men picked up the annoying Jack and sent him away.

"Just you wait, girl. You don't know what's ahead…" he yelled as he fought to be free from the men.

"Thank you," shouted Nick. "Let's get on with the lovely night."

"I'm sorry, Nick, I've ruined your evening."

"No, Abby, you haven't. The night is young and so are we. Would you like to dance?"

"I would," she insisted. Nick led her to the dance floor. She twirled and laughed radiantly. Nick watched her every move so cunning, so sly.

Jack watched them from the back of a ship smoking a cigar. "Abby, Abby, Abby," he said shaking his head. "You've got no idea."

"Oh, Nick," he heard come from her red lips. "Spin me again! Spin me again!" Jack examined her. She was like a child wanting another push on the swing. "Spin me again!" Jack sighed. He stood up to take a walk.

"What time is it, Nick?"

"It's ten forty-five, beautiful."

"Oh my, I must go home. Thank you so very much for the lovely evening. I must be going now."

"Nonsense," Nick demanded. "I'll bring you home. We'll walk."

"What about your party?"

"I was going to leave early anyway. It's no big deal."

"Okay." Abby smiled as she studied him. Nothing was wrong with him, he was a perfect gentleman. The wind blew much harder now. Abby wrapped her cloak around her frigid body tighter. "The winter is coming," Abby said.

"I know. It's been quite cold lately, wouldn't you agree?"

"I do. The summer has been so warm. I almost have forgotten the cold." Nick said nothing.

The two of them walked under the moonlight. The streets were empty. Everyone was inside his or her homes huddling around the fireplace. "I love this time of year. It's the perfect time. Holidays approach us. The winter months roll in. It's a beautiful change."

"I would have to disagree," Nick said sharply.

"Oh?"

"I love the summer…" Nick went raving on how much the summer meant to him. But once again, she blocked him out. *Billy loved the fall, too. He does!* She wanted to shout it out! *Stop concentrating on Billy, Abby,* she thought. *Start concentrating on this gorgeous man.*

As they reached their destination, Abby began listening to Nick again.

"Here we are," Nick reminded. "I wish I had more time with you."

"The same for me, Nick," she agreed truthfully. "Ya' know, maybe there's a way I can meet you after I go in. I'll climb out my window. Meet me…Where?"

"Spring's Tavern. We'll have fun there." Nick was in for it.

"All right. I'll meet you there as soon as I can," Abby said knowing she was breaking Billy's promise.

Abby turned the doorknob and entered the still house. Her family was around the fire and Constance was reading the Bible. "I'm going to bed," Abby said loud and clear. "Good night." Whenever she said, "Good night," no one ever responded.

She continued up the stairs nearly tripping over the cloak, which would have revealed Hattie's dress.

Abby took off the jewelry and returned it to Hattie's box, just in case she would be looking for them later. Then she scurried to her bedroom and opened the large window.

The ground was so far down. Nothing would help her get down safely. She had no sheets because she stuffed them to make it look like she was sleeping in her bed.

What could she use? Abby looked out the window once again. Up and down, left and right. Then an idea came to mind. *If I hang on to the windowpane,* she thought, *I could reach the window on the first floor.*

Abby put one leg out the window, took a deep breath, and put her second leg over. She slid off the ledge and hung onto the pane with her hands. She reached for the window below. If she was a little taller, she could get there perfect. She closed her eyes tight and jumped off. Abby landed on the ground with not a bruise. She lifted herself to her feet and dusted Hattie's dress off. Abby sighed and ran to the tavern.

The pub was mobbed with drunken men who had no lives. *I'm surprised my father isn't here*, she giggled at thought. A few women were there dancing along with the band.

The fiddle sang in harmony along with the banjo strumming its own song. The room was filled with joy and music. Abby walked in and everyone stared at her. She wasn't the kind of girl to be in such a place.

Smoke puffs filled the air. "Have you seen Nick Porter?" she asked a man smoking a long cigarette. He nodded and pointed to the back.

"Thank you," she said trying to spot him. "Nick!" she shouted.

Abby gave up quickly and turned to leave.

"Hey, you," Nick said putting his arm around her waist.

She turned and smiled. "Hi."

"Would you like something to drink? Water…"

"Um…"

"Some beer?" Nick requested.

"Yes," Abby nodded. "Why not?" Nick ordered them two pints. "I've never been in a tavern before," she confessed.

"Well, now you have," Nick grinned handing her the beverage.

"Thank you," she said taking a sip. Abby wanted to spit it out. How awful! The sour taste made her tongue react, but she acted casually.

"You like it?"

"Ah…" she admitted.

"Well, after you have a few more, you'll feel okay." She didn't know what he meant.

The musicians ended their song and began a new one. Just then, Jack went through the door. Abby found him right away.

"Oh God…" Abby shook her head. "He's here, again."

"It's all right. I'll get him."

"Wait!" Abby grabbed his arm before he turned away. "Don't do anything, unless he bothers me. All right?"

"Okay," Nick bargained.

Abby watched as Jack moved through the room slowly. He was coming toward her.

"Why hello, Nicky," a woman teased Nick with a smirk.

"Wendy, this is Abby," he introduced.

Wendy's white face with her red cheeks and a southern accent must attract the men, Abby thought. "Hello, Abby. I've never seen you here before."

"Oh, well I'm just here with Nick," Abby explained as she sipped the bitter beverage.

"Wow! Finally Nicky has a date," she whispered to Abby, but added a wink to Nick. "Nick, we'll talk later, won't we?"

"Yes we will, Wendy."

"Okay then. Well I must get back to my men," she said with a chuckle.

"Bye. Nice meeting you, Wendy…" Abby told her as she ran off to another man.

As soon as Wendy was gone, Jack appeared. "Hello, Abby. Nick."

"Jack…" Abby replied.

"Could I talk to you?" Jack whispered.

"No!" Abby demanded.

"Please?" he pleaded.

"Will you leave me alone?" she asked peering around the room to make sure they weren't making a scene.

"Don't listen to him, Abby," Nick butted in.

"I promise I won't," Jack ignored Nick.

"Excuse me for a second, Nick," she said kindly. Abby led Jack outside to talk. "What is it?"

"What's that?" Jack said pointing to the beer she held in her hand.

" A pint of ale…" Abby said casually.

"Ale? Abby, do you see what he's doing?"

"What?"

"He's getting you drunk," Jack warned.

"So! What if I want to?" Abby giggled as she leaned over to throw up.

"Give it to me!" Jack demanded.

"No!" she shouted as she guzzled down the drink as if it were a potion to save someone's life. "I need a new one," she told Jack.

"Abby…"

"Jack, let me ask you this?" she asked as she pushed the draft to him. "Why are you so concerned about me all of the sudden?"

"Because, Abby, ever since I knew he liked you, I've been worried."

"Worried?" she asked believing none of it. "Are you because Billy told you to be?"

"No…" he shrugged. "No, Abby!"

"You hate me, Jack!" she yelled. "You always did!"

"No I don't!" he rebutted. "Who told you that?"

"Um…" she stuttered. "Actually you did when I was nine."

"What?"

"I remember the day. We were all playing tag and I tagged you. So you told me you hated me."

Jack laughed. "Abby, you were nine. I was eleven! Get it in your head!"

"But I liked you then, Jack," she whined. "I really did."

"Oh, God!" he exclaimed.

"I have to go in now," she pushed away.

"Nick is a jerk, Abby!" he yelled after her.

"Just like you!" she replied. "Nick!" she stumbled. "I want another one!"

"All right!" he handed Abby another pint.

"Thanks, Nicky!" she said laughing as she scoffed more ale down her throat.

"I can tell you never drank before. You're already drunk!"

"And it feels good!" she shouted as she tripped over her own feet. Then the room was spinning. "Oh my God! The room is spinning!" she groaned.

"It's all right," Nick assured. "It will stop soon."

"Are you sure?" she yelled.

"I'm sure," he said rubbing her arms with his hands.

"It stopped," she sighed. Abby was breathing hard.

"Are you all right?" Nick asked with concern.

She took another long sip of the beer. "I'm fine. Can I have another one?"

"Yeah…Can I please have another one?" Nick asked the bartender.

"Yup." The bartender handed Nick another pint.

"Thanks," he told the man quickly.

"Right here!" shouted an angry man as he flipped the table over. "Or are you too chicken to fight a real man, Allen?"

"No way!" Abby shouted as she ran between the two raging men.

"What do you want?" Allen asked furious.

"What's the problem?" she looked at both puzzled faces.

"This man gambled his life savings away and now won't pay

what I have earned. That's what the problem is!" the other stranger snapped.

"Okay then. Don't you think there are other people that have problems, too? If everyone went around fighting, this world would be torn apart."

"So?" Allen asked in a confused tone.

"So…" She didn't know what else to say. "What are you going to gain from fighting? One will be embarrassed because he was beaten up and the other will be proud and tell the whole town. Now tell me," she looked at both the angry men in the eye, "What if you lose? Do you want to be humiliated?" They didn't answer. "That's what I thought. Now…clean up what you did, apologize to one another, and let's get on with our lives. All right?"

"Yes, ma'am."

"Yes, ma'am."

"Thank you." She smiled and walked back to Nick.

"Good job, Abby!" Nick praised.

"Thanks…Can I get another?" she asked the bartender.

"It's on the house," the man behind the bar said. "You saved me a lot of trouble." He handed her another pint of beer.

"Thank you," she smiled.

"You didn't even finish your third," Nick reminded.

"Oh…we can't waste, can we?" She grabbed the mug off the counter where she had left it. She finished it in one mouth full. "There, that's better," she said starting a new one. Abby sighed. "Nick, can we get out of here?"

"Yeah, sure," he agreed with no second thought. They passed through the room and went out the front door into the cold night. "Where do you want to go?"

"I don't know…" She gazed at him and kissed his cheek quickly.

"Abby…What was that for?"

"I don't know," she said confused. "Let's walk. Don't you want to?"

"I'll do anything you want to." They started walking and talking. Nick showed her his house and they stopped there. "Let's go out back…"

"Okay, Nicky," she said delirious. Then in one second, everything went black.

Chapter 6

September 20, 1877

Why didn't Jack stop bothering me? I was getting tired of him. I think I made a good appearance at the party. What do you think, diary? I danced at Nick's party. Then we went to the tavern and...

Billy woke up to the cold morning.

Yesterday, he set his little camp up on the side of the river. He knew he should arrive in Massachusetts soon. He was saying goodbye to Vermont, but he knew he'd be back.

What was Abby doing right now? Thoughts streamed through his head about her and Jack. He stood up and struck a match against his finger. Billy lowered the burning stick down to the logs.

As the fire crackled, he watched the foggy river clear up. Billy took his fishing pole his father had made out of the canoe.

He was going to fish in the Connecticut River!

Billy always wanted to do it, but never had the chance. He knew there was a chance of retrieving nothing because he was on the bank. Billy was hungry and desperate.

He dipped his fishing line into the moving water and waited. Something tugged at his line. Billy lifted it up and gazed at the small fish flapping for freedom. *It was something,* he thought.

Billy cleaned the fish and cooked it over the fire. He was happy he found something to eat, no matter how small it was.

As he was eating, he looked out onto the large river. There was a passing boat. Billy looked at his small canoe and compared it to the larger boat. There was a big difference.

When he finished his small meal, Billy began loading everything back into his canoe. He found a small stream nearby, which was good for water. He filled his canteen up and boarded the little boat.

In a dark alleyway, Abby woke up filthy. She found herself nude and cold. She was scared. Abby didn't remember anything from last night.

Where was she?

Abby dressed herself with Hattie's torn dress. She wrapped herself with her cloak.

She was crying now, wondering what happened to her. Abby knew she would be beaten today for sneaking out last night.

Abby remembered Billy. She could go to him. But, No! He was gone. He would be gone forever.

She started walking toward Main Street, but decided to go behind the buildings. As she turned the corner, rain began falling from the sky. She looked up and saw a gray cloud hanging over the town.

"Abby!" She gasped, for she didn't know who was saying her name. She turned around to see it was Jack.

"Hello, Jack," Abby sniffled.

"What happened to you?" he asked with concern in his voice as he rose from the ground; it was where he slept.

"I don't know!" She busted out with tears.

"Calm down! Sit down!" he demanded with kindness.

"I woke up and I was naked," she told him.

His eyes grew large. "Were you raped?"

"I don't know…The only thing I remember was getting drunk with…Nick. Then I remember going to Spring's Tavern and going to his house. But after, everything went black."

"Nick!" His voice was ragged.

"Yeah, I think I passed out. I'm not sure. But what I'm sure of is that I have a large headache."

Jack sat down next to her and she laid her head down on his chest. "I miss him so much," she whispered.

"Who? Nick?"

"No…Billy. I hope he's okay."

"Me too."

"I like him so much. He had no need to leave. We could have fought them off by ourselves. You know?"

"Yeah, I do."

"How long have you known him?" she asked with curiosity.

"Since we were seven." He laughed. "But I never saw him again after his parents died."

"Oh."

"Sometimes I ran away to find him."

"Really?"

"Yup."

"Well, we can go to his house if you would like to."

"Okay."

"Too bad it's raining."

"It's all right," he shrugged.

"By the way," she asked as they stood up, "why were you here this morning?"

"I passed out, too," he smiled.

Abby laughed. They walked behind the buildings to prevent anyone from seeing them. She was in rags. What if Nick saw her?

Thunder clapped as dark clouds smothered the sky. Lighting struck. The pouring rain invited a cool breeze along. Abby wrapped herself tighter in her cloak.

"Who do you think did this to you?" Jack asked.

"I don't know. But I'm certain it wasn't Nick," she told him.

"Don't be too certain, Abby." Jack shook his head. "He's capable of anything."

"I know," she said with a serious tone. "But I know he didn't. He's a gentleman."

"Oh, yeah, a real man, huh?" Jack was sarcastic.

"Yeah!" she frowned. "A real gentleman. Unlike you were last night."

"Abby, I was only trying to take you away from him! If you had come with me, this wouldn't have happened."

"How do you know?" she stormed.

"I don't, but…can we not discuss me?"

"That would be nice," she agreed. They walked silent for a while. "Do you think Billy will come back?" She looked up at him with worried eyes.

"Yes," he lied. He didn't know.

"Good," she smiled assured.

They arrived at the store and started walking toward the path.

"It's gorgeous," she said. "I love it there. It's home to me."

"Can't wait to see it." They came upon the rushing river. Jack and Abby entered the old canoe.

"My God, I hope the Connecticut River isn't dangerous," she worried.

"I'm sure he's fine, Abby. Don't worry."

"Right…" she reminded herself. Abby stood up and pushed the boat along the river with Billy's pole.

She sat down and placed his pole in the boat. As they were drifting down the river, Abby gazed at the familiar sights. The leaves on the trees were turning a lot more. The rain made the river displeasure to the eyes. Surely, Jack would think she'd been lying to him.

Abby closed her eyes and when she opened them, she hoped she would be at Old Mann Rock. There were good memories there and she wanted to remember them.

As they approached the rock, Abby was embarrassed. Where had all the magic gone? Billy was the heaven, which touched down to Earth.

"Oh my," Abby's cheeks turned crimson, "Old Mann Rock is in bad shape today."

"Nah," Jack said attempting to make her feel better. "It's lovely."

They departed the boat and climbed the rock. The rain stopped for a while back, but began falling hard to the ground.

Abby sat down on the large stone. "You know…" she stared into space as she spoke. "When it used to rain, we'd still swim. It was fun. Then every time it was cloudy, we couldn't see the sunset. We always watched the sunset together. Anyway, when there was no sunset to be seen, we'd sit on the rock with our feet hanging over the edge. Billy and I would think and not talk."

Abby's face was dripping wet and Jack sat down next to her to hear her story. "I always wondered what he was thinking. I thought about how good his life was here and how good mine was when I was here, too.

God knows what Billy thought. Maybe he thought about that day or the sunset behind the clouds. Or he could have thought about his departure from…me…" By now, her tears dribbled down her face.

Jack saw her pain. She was out of it. "Come on," he patted her hand. "Let's go to his house and get warm. I'll make a fire."

Abby nodded. "That would be nice." She stood up with Jack's hand and headed toward the path. Again, they said nothing to each other. Silence overcame them like the stormy clouds overhung the town.

When Jack saw Billy's house, there was a sudden awe on his face. Something about that house made it sparkle and shine, even in the worse weather.

"Isn't it gorgeous?" she questioned.

Jack said nothing. He just looked at the house. Abby was amused. "Come on," she giggled. "Let's go inside."

"Hmmmm…" Abby said looking around the clean house. "Billy must've tidied up before he left."

"Why? Was it messy?" Jack wondered.

"No…" she said with a smirk. "It didn't look like this yesterday."

"Oh…"

Abby sat down on the loveseat where Christina sat yesterday and rubbed the empty seat next to her where Billy kissed her. A tear flowed down her cheek.

She wiped it away to be strong. "So…Where's that fire you promised?"

"Oh…" He had forgotten. "I'll go get some wood." He left the room and went outside.

As soon as the door shut behind him, Abby ran upstairs to Billy's bedroom. She flopped herself onto his small bed. Abby noticed there was no quilt on it. She closed her eyes and took a deep breath.

What happened to me? Life was never like this. It was so simple and good. I never worried about anything. All of those thoughts scrambled around her head.

"Abby! Abby! Where are you?" Jack's voice bellowed for her.

Abby jumped up and scurried to the top of the staircase. She ran downstairs. "I'm right here!" she shouted as she jumped from the last step.

"Oh…Well, I made your fire."

"Thank you."

"He has a nice house."

"I know," she agreed while she sat down in a chair. "Oh! I've been meaning to ask you, how's your mother?"

"I don't know," he was calm as he sat in the loveseat. "The doctor doesn't know either."

"Oh really?" she was sympathetic.

"Yeah…And he said she doesn't have much time."

"I'm so sorry, Jack."

"It's okay. She seems to have been sick my whole life. She suffers."

Abby smiled and became dazed in the fire. "Your mother is a great woman. She was a great teacher, even when she was sick. She taught me a lot. I think that's why I love to read so much."

"Yeah…" Jack agreed. The rain clattered on the windowpane and the thunder roared as if it was a lion guarding its jungle against poachers. The day looked like night with the dark clouds hanging over Vermont.

"Oh, it's so cold now. Summer just flew by as if it were nothing at all," Jack agreed. Silence came over both of them. They thought about completely different things.

"Do you think you should go home?" Jack suggested.

"If I go home…" she was worried. "If I go home, I don't know what's going to happen.

"What do you mean?"

"I mean, I snuck out last night and I didn't go back home. I'm staying out too late."

"Tell them what happened."

"I can't, Jack. You don't understand."

"Understand, what? You woke up this morning in an alleyway. What isn't there to understand, Abby?"

"My father beats me," she whispered.

"He what?"

"He…beats me. There's nothing I can do about it, either."

"Oh…" Jack looked stunned. "I'm sorry."

"It's all right," she said to him. "I do have to go home."

"We both should. I have to check on my mom."

"Okay. Besides, I promised Billy I'd try to stay out of my father's way."

Jack smiled as he rose from his seat.

"I'll get some water from the pump outside."

"I'll do it," Jack insisted.

"Jack, let me do something," she snapped.

"All right, if you want to."

Abby ventured out the back door to the water pump. It wasn't very far. She set down her pail underneath the faucet.

Abby started pumping, but after a few times, she stopped. She thought she heard something in the distance. Abby started to pump once more. The noise came closer as she pumped faster. Her arm was tired and helpless, but she didn't care.

When the water reached the top, she ran fast, but carefully, inside. Water spilled out of the small bucket.

Abby poured the water on the fire and bolted out the door, saying nothing to Jack. He ran after her.

"Abby! Abby, wait!" She ran all the way to the rock and boarded the boat. Jack caught her before she pushed off. "What's wrong?"

"I heard…" she panted. "I heard noises."

"Noises? What kind of noises?" he was stunned.

"People noises. I'm not sure." She was terrified. Jack jumped into the boat as Abby poled off.

Rain began to fall from the sky. Lightning lit up the horizon with distant claps of thunder. Billy never thought about this situation. He stopped paddling for a minute, but began to start again. Through the fog and rain, he saw boats lined up on shore. He would stop there until the storm came to an end.

Billy strolled the streets of the unknown town. He walked up the few steps of a building and decided to enter. Not knowing how to read and write was hard. Billy took a chance and went in.

As soon as he walked in, he knew it was a bank. Billy walked up to the teller. "Where's the nearest tavern?" Billy inquired.

"Around the corner, sir," the old man responded with his eyes down at the money he was counting. The man's bushy gray brows shaded his eyes the way trees protect the earth in a forest.

Billy turned and left to go have a pint of beer. The streets were a bit crowded as he meandered around the corner.

He entered the pub filled with smoke and men. Billy walked slowly toward the front of the tavern.

"I'll have some ale, please," Billy requested.

"Yup," the bartender said. Billy looked around.

"Hey, stranger," an older woman teased as she went behind the bar. "I've never seen you around here before."

"Well, I'm not from here," Billy smiled.

"Where ya' from?" the bartender questioned as he handed him a pint of ale.

"Vermont. I'm traveling down to Connecticut."

"Well, you've got a ways," the done-up woman told him busily with her orders.

"I know."

"Well, welcome to Greenfield. I'm Linda." Linda went back to her customers.

Billy sat down on one of the stools. "Where in Connecticut?" the middle-aged bartender wondered aloud.

"I'm not sure. I know there's no way I'm going on the ocean with my little canoe?"

"I know it," the man chimed. "I grew up in Enfield, Connecticut."

"Really? Where's that about?'

"It's on the river," he assured. "It's a nice area. It's the first stop in Connecticut. There's a covered bridge as you enter the town. There's work there. They make gunpowder and such."

"Good..." Billy said as he sipped the last of his beer.

"Want another one, baby?" Linda asked. "It's on me."

"Sure," Billy smiled. "I'm here until the storm's over."

"Well, then, ya' might as well have a few more."

"Maybe I will," he smirked.

"Okay, then," the bartender said as he handed Billy a pint.

"When's the storm gonna be over?" Billy asked.

"Dunno. Probably soon." Billy looked around the pub as he sipped his beverage again. "Listen…" the man whispered. Billy leaned in to hear. "There's a rumor spreading around Greenfield that there are Indians down river."

"Indians?" he was bewildered. He remembered Abby telling him something about them.

"Ya' know, redskins?" the man rolled his eyes. "Are you telling me you've got no clue what Indians are?"

"Oh, yeah." Billy tried to act as if he did, although he didn't know.

"Well, I hear they're real bad now. Just to warn you."

"Thanks." Billy was relieved he was warned. He took his last sip and placed the beverage holder on the surface. "I have to be going now. Seems to me, the storm's cleared up." The two men shook hands and Billy turned to leave.

"Goodbye, Linda," Billy said leaving the tavern.

"Bye…" She recalled that she didn't know his name. "What's your name?"

"Billy, ma'am."

"Well, goodbye, Billy. Have a safe trip." She smiled and continued her work.

Billy stepped outside and shook his head. "Indians?" He walked back toward the wide river.

As he hopped into his canoe, the sun poked through the clouds leaving rays of golden sunlight. Hawks flew over the river rejoicing the storm was over and they were now free.

Billy began to paddle and feel an emotion he had not felt on his journey yet. It was the fear of Indians. What were they like? Are they as bad as the bartender said?

OLD MANN ROCK

The water was moving fast, but Billy kept the boat in control. Paddling with one person was hard. After all, he had never done it before. Billy always used his pole with Abby. The water was much too deep to use the pole now.

Billy searched the horizon for any sign of Indians with his tired eyes. What did they look like? Before he left his house, he brought with him his father's rifle, which was now tucked safely under his seat. Hopefully, it would protect him.

Abby opened the back door of her house. She peeked her head around the door to see if anyone was there. The kitchen was empty. She tiptoed inside and up the old stairs to her bedroom.

First, she took off the rags she wore and put them back into Hattie's trunk. Then, she went to her bedroom. Abby, naked as she found herself that morning, put on a dress.

It felt good to have a new dress on. She brushed her straggly hair and braided it.

Abby saw her bed hadn't been touched. They didn't know she was gone! No one had bothered to wake her for breakfast. She wouldn't be beaten today. She laughed for they were foolish.

Abby decided to go back out and look for Nick.

She walked Main Street acting as normal as ever. Abby went to Nick's house and knocked on the door. Christina answered to her knock.

"Hello, Abby," she chimed. "What can I do for you?"

"Could I please see Nick?" Abby asked.

"Sure you can. Come right in," she invited. Abby stepped inside the gloomy house.

Nick came out of a room handsomely dressed. "Abby!" he was surprised to see her.

"Hi, Nick. How are you?" Abby asked.

"Good. You?" he responded. Christina went into the room, which Nick had left.

"I'm okay. Since the storm's over, would you walk with me?" she asked kindly.

63

"Sure." Abby turned and went out the door, with Nick following her. "What's the matter, Abby?" he questioned closing the door behind him.

They started walking. "Last night…" she was choked up. What if he did rape her? Would he admit it? "Well…this morning, I found myself…naked…in an alleyway."

"Are you okay?" Nick asked concerned.

"I remember nothing from last night."

"Nothing?"

"No…everything went black."

"Well…when we came to my house…"

She cut his sentence off. "That's when it happened."

"You told me you needed to go home. I said I'd bring you, but you insisted on going alone. So, I let you go alone. That's the last time I saw you."

Abby wanted to cry. Was he lying? But he seemed so convincing.

"Thanks, Nick. I have to go!" she rushed.

"Bye, Abby." She ran off toward Jack's house.

When she reached his house, she knocked on the door loudly. Jack answered.

"Abby?"

"Jack, I need to talk to you."

"Not now. I'm busy."

"It's about Billy."

"What?" he was aggravated and didn't want to hear it now.

"Why did he leave?" she was almost in tears.

"The killers were back, Abby! That's why!"

"Why after all these years? How did he know?" Jack put the pieces together. He ran out the front door toward the river.

"Come on. We're going to Old Mann Rock!" She ran after him.

Jack boarded the boat so quickly he almost broke it. Abby hopped in seconds later.

"You heard noises?" Jack asked impatiently poling down the river.

"Yeah. It occurred to me somehow when I was talking to Nick."

"You talked to him?" Jack's voice was raging.

"To ask him about last night."

"And…"

"And he said I went home alone and nothing happened."

"God, Abby! Anyone would say that! How dumb can you be?"

"I'm not dumb at all. I believe him, Jack!" He was furious, as he shook his head. "Let's not talk about this anymore, please?"

"You're the one who brought it up," he argued.

"I had to tell you where I had the idea from," she rebutted.

They approached the rock and bolted to the path in the woods. No one was there, but the door was wide open. They went in.

"Someone was here," Abby said.

"I know, but who?" Jack thought aloud. "What if it was Nick?"

"Jack!" she snapped. "It wasn't Nick! Just shut up!"

Jack sighed. "I thought someone would be here."

"Me too. That's why I went to you. I didn't want to be alone." Abby went upstairs to see Billy's bedroom. Jack followed her.

"It wasn't like this when I was here this morning," Abby said frantically. "There's something different about it."

"Maybe because there was someone here for sure." Jack picked up a gun from Billy's bed. "Was this here when you were?"

"No…" she was stunned.

"Put it somewhere, just in case they, or she or he, comes back." Jack handed her the gun.

"Okay…" She looked around the room. Abby opened the top drawer of Billy's dresser and placed the gun there.

"Do you know how to use it?" Jack asked.

"Oh, yeah," she lied. "Let's get out of here."

"My pleasure," Jack agreed. Both of them, feeling bewildered, went downstairs and through the front door.

They proceeded to the rock and went into the boat.

"Jack, I've got a question," Abby started.

"Yeah?" he said, poling down river.

"Why were you so busy when I went to get you?"

Jack didn't answer right away. He grinned. "I had a special girl in the house who will need a big apology for my absence."

"Who?"

"Why should I tell you?" he teased.

"Please? Is she your girlfriend?"

"I'd like her to be." He couldn't stop smiling.

"Tell me. I won't tell anyone," Abby promised.

"Sarah Bridge," he confessed.

She gasped. "Are you serious? She's so nice."

"I know."

"Well, I'm happy for you."

"Thanks, Abby."

"I can't believe you like the doctor's daughter."

"The doctor's her father?" Jack said seriously.

Abby laughed. "Yeah. Doctor Bridge, Jack."

"Well, he's mean!" Jack was defensive.

"Believe me, he'll like you."

"I can't believe that Sarah's father's the doctor."

"Believe it," Abby said.

"I don't know what to say."

"Don't say anything," Abby chuckled.

Chapter 7

September 30, 1877

Can you believe what has happened to me? I've been raped and Billy might have lied to me. But why? Why did he have to leave? There must be a reason why...after all these years he packs up and goes off like this? Hopefully he'll come back and that will be the first question out of my mouth. Unless, of course, Jack and I can figure it out first.

Love,
Abby

These stars were as beautiful as the ones at home, Billy thought. Days passed and Billy hadn't seen any Indians. He was grateful he hadn't. Just in case they came, Billy kept his gun next to him while he slept during the day.

With his lantern lit and Billy paddling down river, the cool breeze of winter soared the river like an eagle glided in the sky.

Billy thought about what this place, Enfield, what would be like. *Was it as good as the man behind the bar said it was? Or was it different?*

Nights on the river were peaceful. There were no ships bringing cargo to the ports. Sometimes Billy would drift down, watching the stars. Once in a great while he would see a few shooting stars. He would make a wish when he saw one fly by. Usually, they were about Abby. But sometimes they would be about staying out of the Indians' way.

Big clouds rolled in from the north and laid rain on the Earth. It was hard to see where he was heading when it poured. Now was the time to stop for the night.

Billy paddled to the side, and observed a dim light in the distance. *He would stop and make peace*, he thought.

As he reached the side, Billy noticed they looked different than the men where he lived. They had darker skin and longer hair with beads around their necks and feathers in their hair. Could they be Indians?

Billy was fearful of what they might do, so he tried to escape, but he already caught the attention of one of them. He said something, but it wasn't English.

"Hello," an Indian said with a deep accent.

"Hello," Billy replied.

"Would you like to sit with us?" the man said as Billy was about to reach for his gun. He decided not to reach for the weapon.

"Yes."

"Sit down, boy!" the Indian demanded. Billy obeyed quickly. He sat down.

"What's your name?"

"Billy," he choked. "My name's Billy."

"In your foreign language my name is Tree Rattles. This is our chief." He pointed to the man, whom had the largest headdress. "You can call him Chief."

"Okay."

"This is Howling at Moon," Tree Rattles told Billy. "The last man is Blue Sky."

"Hello to you all," Billy said. Tree Rattles translated what Billy had said.

"Hello, is what they say."

"What are you good men doing on the river?" Billy questioned.

"We are going down East Coast." The accent was so deep in Tree Rattles' voice, Billy almost couldn't understand his words. "You?"

"I'm stopping in Connecticut. Probably Enfield, Connecticut."

"Enfield, Connecticut one day away." Billy was certainly glad to hear that. A new life was ahead of him. He smiled.

That night, the five men sat around the fire trading certain things. With his money, Billy bought a bead necklace for Abby, just in case he went back home one day.

Billy slept by the fire and in the morning, he ate a hearty breakfast with his new friends. The smoky fire filled the trees around them with big gray clouds. The sun rising on the water made the river appear almost as glass.

He said goodbye to the Indians, packed up his belongings and left to get to Enfield. Billy was determined to get there that day.

As he paddled down the river, he thought how very wrong the bartender had been about the Indians. *Maybe they're not all like that? Hopefully the man who served the pints of ale wasn't wrong about Enfield.*

What would he do there? Where would he stay? Did he have enough money? What would his life be like? Billy had no answers. He was puzzled at his own questions. The morning fog lifted from the water and Billy could see what was ahead clearly now. Billy wondered if he would miss the river. Would he miss the anxiety of going somewhere where there's no telling what would happen? He wasn't sure once again.

Paddling the long day was hard. Everyday, Billy would wonder about seeing Abby's face. *Was she still mad at him? What if he came back and she didn't want to see him again?*

Those ideas didn't even cross his mind when he left. Billy hoped that she wasn't so mad at him, that now she's seeing Nick.

Dusk came and there was no sign of Enfield. Maybe the Indians were wrong. Billy wasn't tired, so he wouldn't stop for the night.

The moon was full and big. Billy stared at it for a while. He sighed. He was tired of the river. He just wanted to get to Enfield and live a normal life.

Suddenly, Billy was startled at what he saw. He saw lights and a bridge. There was a covered bridge! He was in Enfield. Billy jumped for joy. He was so happy, he almost tipped the boat.

"Yes!" he shouted. Billy wanted the whole world to hear him. He made it! The Indians were right!

He happily rowed to the right side of the river and went on shore.

Billy tied his rope around a tree and set out to find a hotel. Billy wasn't quite sure of the tall buildings. He walked on the dirt road, which seemed to be Main Street.

Then, after walking quite a ways away from the river, he saw a large building with buggies and stagecoaches outside. He thought it must have been a hotel. Billy decided to check it out.

With money in his pocket to spend, he climbed the stoop. The room he entered was filled with elegant men and women. Billy knew it was a hotel.

"Welcome to the Hazardville Hotel," the man behind the counter greeted Billy as he approached it.

"Thank you, sir."

"Can I help you?"

"Yes. Could I have a room for tonight?"

"Yes, sir. You're in luck. We have one more room available."

"Great." Billy was happy. The man said the price of the room and Billy gave him all his money. The clerk looked stunned and figured Billy wasn't educated.

He handed Billy a key. "Your room is 21."

"Thank you." The number was engraved in the key, so Billy could match it up with the number on the door.

Billy went out the front door, to retrieve his belongings. He didn't have much. Billy would bring his gun for sure, just in case someone decided to steal it.

As he walked back to the Hazardville Hotel with his things, he decided Enfield was a nice town. Billy would like it here. The small city was lit up with much nightlife in the taverns. Billy wouldn't visit them today because he was too tired.

Billy's boots made a loud racket as he climbed the stairs. He searched the doors for his room. Indeed, he found number twenty-one. Billy slipped the key in he hole and twisted it. He turned the doorknob.

The room was small, but comfortable. A small round table lay in the far right corner with two chairs next to it. A kerosene lantern was neatly placed there and was already lit. The wallpaper was a floral ray of flowers and made the room cozy. The big bed took up much room and was high, just like the one belonging to his parents. The quilt on it was big and full of feathers. The view of the town was perfect; the hotel was on the corner of two streets.

Billy set his treasures down and locked his door. There was ice and water in a pitcher waiting for his dry mouth. He poured himself a glass and drank the water slowly, savoring every gulp.

He turned the sheets of the bed over and slipped inside them after removing his boots. The bed felt good. After all, the bank of the river and the canoe wasn't a good bed.

It began to rain outside and Billy laughed. He was so happy he wasn't on the river. As the thunder pierced the sky with its fierce cry, Billy lay in his bed too excited to fall asleep.

Tomorrow he would look for a job and find somewhere to stay temporarily. He didn't have much money left, he knew for sure.

Billy closed his tired eyes and went to sleep.

The sun rays tried to peek through the curtains that hung. It wasn't too long after dawn, travelers from who-knows-where were moving in the hallways. Children shouted as they ran up and down the stairs with their parents trying to keep them quiet.

Billy didn't mind it. He was actually fascinated by the people. After all, for almost his whole life he stayed at Old Mann Rock.

He pulled himself out of bed and slipped his muddy boots back on. Billy picked up his money from the small table and headed out for breakfast.

In the small restaurant downstairs, Billy sat at a small table and waited for his waiter.

To his surprise, a waitress appeared at his table. "What would you like, boy?" The lady was crabby.

"Could I have some coffee and some bread with butter please?"

"Sure you can," she responded, trying to sound friendly. After she left, Billy twiddled his thumbs for he had no idea what to do. He sighed. What could he do for an occupation? He couldn't read or write. He had no skills.

The woman came back with Billy's bread and coffee. "Thank you," Billy said.

"Yeah, you're welcome." She slapped a piece of paper down on the table.

"How much is this bill?" Billy was embarrassed.

The rude woman rolled her eyes and walked away.

"Are you telling me, boy, you don't know how to read?" spoke an older woman.

Billy turned to see a frail woman, who was as white as snow. "It's true, ma'am."

The woman slowly walked to Billy's table and sat down in the chair across from him. "Tell me…Why not?"

"I was never educated," he responded quite quickly.

"Well, then…" She put her own money on the table as Billy ate his breakfast. "Come on, boy."

"But…"

"There are no buts…"

"I didn't finish," he whined as he stuffed more bread in his mouth. Billy followed her outside.

"Where are we going?" he asked.

"To my house…"

"Where's that?"

"You'll see." They took a quick left as they entered another street. There was a big hill sloping toward a smaller river than the Connecticut. The woman went a few hundred yards, then turned onto her stone path.

"Is this your house?" Billy whispered.

"Indeed…You can stay with me."

"Thank you."

"Sure, boy. You look like you're in need. Where are you from?" she asked opening the front door of her small house.

"I'm from Vermont."

"Where in Vermont?"

"I don't know. This is Enfield, Connecticut, right?"

"Yes," she assured him. "Now, why are you here?"

Billy didn't want to answer. "My parents, when I was nine, were murdered."

"Oh, my," she gasped.

"Their murderers are coming back and I didn't want to stay around there."

The house was cozy. It was clean and a fire was lit. The wooden floors creaked as they walked around. Two rocking chairs were around the fire. Lace curtains were decorating the windows just like his house. He liked it here.

"Oh. Well, what's your name? I forgot to ask you that."

"Billy Sanson."

"Well, Billy, I'm Elizabeth Rother. Nice to meet you." They shook hands.

"Elizabeth was my mother's name." Billy smiled.

"You can call me Liz, though."

"Okay."

"Do you have any belongings?"

"Yes, they're back at the hotel."

"You go get them and I'll bake us supper for tonight."

"Okay." Billy let himself out the front door and walked toward the hotel. *What a nice lady*, he thought.

As he approached the building at the corner, he saw a man yelling with papers in his hands.

"Do you need a job?" he raved. "Well if you do, you're in luck!" the man handed a flyer to Billy when he walked by.

Billy climbed the stoop with joy on his face. He went inside the hotel and climbed the stairs. He reached in his pocket for the room key to unlock the door. Billy twisted the doorknob and went inside.

He picked up his belongings and exited the room, shutting the door behind him. When he was on the first floor again, Billy returned the key to the front desk.

Billy stepped outside and the man, who was advertising the job, was gone. Billy started back to Liz's house.

The town was awake and already bustling when Abby awoke.

She stretched her arms and noticed Constance wasn't in bed. Abby hoped they ate breakfast without her. She wasn't hungry.

Abby lifted her nightgown over her head and slipped on her dress. It was dirty, but she didn't care. She combed her long hair and put on Billy's mother's necklace. Every morning she would hold it tight and say a prayer for Billy.

Abby ran down the stairs. There was no one there. She suddenly remembered today was Sunday. They were at church.

She slipped out the back door to go to the rock. The leaves were radiant colors as they shone in the bright sun. It was a beautiful day with the blue sky spilling to the horizon. The cool day made Abby wish she had her cloak.

Abby poled down the river in the cold, clear water. The rock was more beautiful than ever. She climbed the large boulder and sat on the cold surface with her feet dangling over the side.

She sighed. What was next? What did God have in store for the future? Abby laid down on the rock to look up at the sky.

Hawks circled the forest, peering in every direction to spot prey. She was scared. What if the murderers came back today? What would she do? Then, she remembered the gun in Billy's drawer upstairs. She didn't know how to use it. Hopefully she wouldn't need it.

Abby climbed to her feet and walked to the path. She opened the big wooden door to the house and went inside.

Abby walked to the library door and invited herself into the wonderful room. The sunlight shone on the books. It was as if each ray was requesting a different book to Abby.

She ran her fingers over the old bindings and then went to the table in the middle of the room. Abby picked up a book with a beat-up leather cover. She opened it. Inside, on the first page, it read:

Journal of Gregory Sanson
Civil War
1861

Today I am departing from my beloved family. I don't know if I will return to them. My son, Billy, is only one years old. My wife is a young woman of seventeen and I fear I will not be able to kiss her tender lips ever again. I have made a home, in which is safe for them to live. It's out of harm's way. I must stop writing now. I feel tears running down my cheeks.

Abby's eyes were big. She couldn't believe she held in her hands the journal of Billy's father. Maybe it stated a clue why they were murdered.

Abby sat herself in a chair and looked quickly through the papers on the table. She didn't know what the documents were for. Abby sighed.

The wind was howling outside. The house was cold and bare, too. Abby took herself out of the seat and went into the kitchen. She looked around for a reason she didn't know and continued walking to the stairs.

When she reached Billy's bedroom, she looked around again. Abby had no idea why her body was doing that. A chill ran down her spine, for she was scared now.

Abby opened the top drawer of Billy's dresser and saw that the gun was gone. Was someone here? Abby didn't move, but her eyes darted all over the room.

She turned around to see behind her. No one was there. Abby had a bad feeling.

She found the gun on the bed where Jack had found it before. As she picked it up, another racing chill ran down her back. Abby felt she was not alone. She dropped the gun into her pocket in her dress and for the third time, looked around again.

It was only her head. These thoughts were only in her head, she hoped. Was her gut telling her something? Abby wished she knew what it was telling her. They spoke totally different languages.

Abby wondered if Billy's mother was ever scared to be alone like Abby was at the moment. Abby's hands shook in fear. She reminded herself there was nothing to be scared of. Her nerves ignored the reminder.

Abby grasped the gun in her hand to make her feel safer, but it didn't work. She started downstairs and opened the front door to go outside.

She needed to breathe fresh air. Abby sat in one of the rocking chairs on the porch. She rocked in it slowly.

Abby looked out, and if she saw a small movement like a squirrel she would jump. Abby took the gun out of her pocket to see how to work it. Why didn't it come with instructions? She put it back in her large pocket.

The sun was high in the sky and she thought it was about noon. The wind clapped at the windows. Her hair blew in the gentle breeze. Abby squinted her eyes trying to see beyond the trees. It wasn't a possibility.

Abby went to one of the flower boxes, which hung under the windows, and gathered a bouquet of them in her hand. She walked the path to Old Mann Rock. When she was there, Abby stood on the rock and waited. She waited for the wind.

When the North Wind rolled in, Abby held her arm out, over the water and let go of the flowers. As she watched them flow gently in the wind, Abby recited the, *"Our Father."*

"Amen," she ended. "Please God let me be safe." Abby sighed. When all the flowers were out of sight, Abby turned to visit Mr. and Mrs. Sanson's grave.

The flag waved proudly in the breeze and Abby knelt down to recite yet another *"Our Father."*

"…Amen," she ended again. "Please Mr. and Mrs. Sanson, let me be safe as well as your beloved son." A tear crashed down Abby's face. It was meaningless.

Abby stood up and went to the path. She continued toward the house and stopped at the garden when she reached it. There were ripe tomatoes, so she picked them. Abby ate one as if it were an apple. *The tomato was so juicy and good,* she thought.

Abby didn't want to go inside the house, but she had to face her fears. She opened the door slowly and peeked her head in. The coast was clear. She proceeded inside.

The icebox was empty. She didn't care, though. Abby ate the rest of her tomatoes and was full.

Sunset was arriving the world. Abby went to the rock again to watch it go down.

She sat upon it and the beautiful sky had her wishing Billy were next to her. The sunset wasn't an ordinary setting. It seemed magical.

Once Abby thought about it, there wasn't one sunset exactly the same. They were all beautiful and unique in their own way.

It was like people in a way. Somehow, there was something beautiful and unique about each and every person on this world. Abby excluded her parents.

She thought about her sisters. She loved them very much. Even though they were spoiled and ignored her, there wasn't anything really wrong with them. They were beautiful and very unique in very different ways.

No one on this Earth was the same. They couldn't be if they tried. Life for everyone was different. Abby tried to smile. No one on Earth knew how she was feeling right now.

When the sun was set behind the mountains, Abby went back to Billy's house.

She lit a lantern that she found in Billy's bedroom with matches she discovered next to the fireplace in the living room.

The night sky overcame the horizon and left Abby walking around with the lantern in her hand to find her way. She climbed the stairs to go to Billy's bedroom. Although she was still scared, she now felt she was alone. Abby was relieved.

She placed the lantern on the floor and sunk into Billy's bed. Abby closed her eyes for a while. The North wind blew inside from the opened windows. The flame flickered.

In one second, rain poured from the sky. Abby loved hearing the rain at night while she slept. She took a deep breath.

"Where are you boy?" a man stormed as he barged through the door. Abby's eyes opened in a half of a second.

"Maybe he's gone," a woman said.

"Nah. When I came here yesterday I saw some movement through the trees," another man said.

Abby jumped up and hid the lit lantern in the closet to hide the glow of the bright flame.

They're here! They're here! That's all she thought about as she looked for a place to hide.

Abby looked out the window. She heard footsteps coming up the stairs. She bolted for the window and climbed out onto the roof. Abby hid with her back straight against the house, between the two windows.

Abby was in shock. She panted loudly, but tried to breathe quieter. She heard the trio come in Billy's bedroom.

"There's my gun," one of the two men said. Abby noticed the gun she was carrying must've fallen out of her pocket onto the bed.

Abby swallowed hard and closed her eyes tight. She heard the closet door open.

"Someone's here," the woman observed.

"There is. He ain't gonna get away, either. We've got to finish the family off," an angry man said.

Abby felt her body begin to slip, but she held on to the window with her fingers. In the corner of her eye, she saw the glow of her lantern leave the room. She took a deep breath. Abby said another, "*Our Father,*" but to herself this time.

From where Abby hid, she heard doors opening, papers rustling, and cabinets opening from the murderers. There wasn't a doubt in her mind that said the trio wasn't the killers of Billy's parents.

For some strange reason, Abby recognized the voices, but was too frightened to think of who they were.

The rain was making the roof and the window wet. Again, she began to slip. Abby tried not to move.

With the three of them searching for Billy, they combed the house through quickly.

"Damn!" one of the men said with an angry tone. "The boy's not here!"

"Don't worry, he can't stay wherever he is for long."

"But the boat's here…"

"Doesn't mean he's here," the woman reminded. They went

outside and slammed the door behind them.

She only saw the glow moving because of the fog and rain in the air.

When the glow was gone, Abby quickly climbed back in the house. She ran down the stairs in the pitch black. Abby ran all the way to the rock without stopping and pushed the boat rapidly on the river.

As she poled through the water as quickly as she could, she started thinking about the familiar voices. She couldn't help but cry, when she realized who they were.

The pouring rain filled the streets. Only a few carriages were on the street as Abby paced through.

As she approached Jack's house, she could only think of the murderers. Abby was in the state of shock.

"Jack! Jack!" she cried as she pounded on his door. Jack opened it and his eyes grew large at the sight of his wet friend.

"Abby? Come in! Come in!" Jack led Abby inside and shut the door. "What's wrong?"

She tried to catch her breath. Jack knew there was something terribly the matter.

"Abby, what's wrong?" he demanded an answer as he shook her on his shoulders.

"I know..."

"Know what?"

"I know who the..." she burst into tears.

"What, Abby?"

"I know who killed Billy's parents," she finally said.

"Who?" Jack asked looking at her with deep sorrow. "Tell me, Abby. Who are the killers?"

"The killers are..." she couldn't say it. The words weren't there yet. "The killers are my parents."

Chapter 8

October 2, 1877

> *Today is the second of October! I am now scared to go back home. But I must. I have nowhere to stay. I was in shock when I found out about the murderers. I feel so bad. Why would they kill Billy's parents? I need to find out the truth. I wonder if Billy knew they were the ones?*

> *Abby*

Billy opened the door to the small house and went inside. Liz was preparing a meal for the both of them.

"Look what I have found," Billy praised as he handed the wise woman the flyer.

"A job, Billy? Well, you certainly are a motivated boy, aren't you?"

"I guess," he smiled. "What does it say?"

"It says:

Private Mail Carrier for Hazard Powder.
No experience of horses are necessary."

"Hazard Powder? What's that?" Billy wasn't sure if this was a great idea.

"It's the gunpowder industry. It was a big supplier for the Civil War."

"My father fought in that war. He used to tell me all about it."

"Did he come out of it all right?" Liz asked quietly.

"Yes, he did."

"Not everyone did."

"Oh, I know," he shrugged.

"My husband and son never came back from that war."

"Oh, Liz, I'm so sorry," Billy was sympathetic.

"My son was only twenty-five. Only a few years older than you," her voice was hurt and confused. "You actually remind me a lot of Peter." Billy knew that this woman was lonely. No wonder she took him in with no regrets. "The war was an awful thing. So many lives and families were shattered."

"I can imagine. I was only one year old when he went off."

"Imagine if your father never came back. Imagine your mother raising you alone."

"How awful."

"You're right."

"Now, everyday people are killing each other. Let's just hope it doesn't get worse in the future."

"I hope it doesn't."

"You must be such a good boy at home. Where you come from."

"I guess there are better," Billy said.

"So, tell me about your story." Liz wanted to know. He didn't know where to start. *Should he talk about Abby?* He thought that would be a good idea.

"There's a special girl where I come from," Billy started.
"What's her name?"

"Abby…"

"Abby!"

"Huh?" she was in daze.

Jack handed her a hot mug. Abby was wrapped in a big blanket next to the roaring fire.

"Are you okay?" Jack asked.

"Yeah…I'm fine now."

"Jack?" Jack's mother came out from a bedroom door.

"Oh, Ma…it's okay. It's only Abby."

Tessa Canning walked slowly and Abby knew she was in great pain. Tessa was blind. "Oh, Abby dear, how are you?"

"I'm okay…how about you? You seem to be getting better."

"Do I?" She was a hopeful lady. Abby respected her so much.

"I only wish I could be in the classroom again, teaching you."

"I don't go to school anymore," Abby filled her in with the recent news.

"Oh, really? That's a shame. You were my brightest student," she complemented.

"Thank you. That's nice to hear," Abby said appreciatively.

"I only speak the truth, my dear."

"Ma, maybe you can help us," Jack spoke up.

"With what, Jack?"

"Abby…she has a friend," Jack began to explain.

"Did you ever know Elizabeth and Gregory Sanson?" Abby questioned.

"Oh, yes…Jack was friends with his son…"

"Well, his name is Billy. Eight years ago, Elizabeth and Gregory were murdered." Abby just said it. There was no stuttering involved.

Tessa gasped. "How sad! Why didn't we ever hear about it?"

"Because they live on the river and no one knew. Billy grew up by himself. Actually, when I was ten, we met and I went to his house everyday."

Tessa listened carefully.

"Tonight…I found out who the murderers were. See, Billy left his house and went down the Connecticut River because he said that the murderers were back."

"We're wondering how he knew," Jack added.

"But, Abigail, who are the murderers?"

"I am so ashamed. You won't tell anyone…"

"I promise."

"My parents…"

Tessa gasped once more. "Oh my. How awful."

"I know. I'm so afraid to go back home. I'm afraid my father will beat me again," Abby's voice was interrupted by the pain she felt in her heart.

"He beats you?" Tessa was in shock.

"Yes."

"I knew they shouldn't have taken you," Tessa said.

"What do you mean?" Abby was bewildered.

"Oh, someone must've told you..."

"Told me what?" Abby wasn't sure if it was a wonderful or horrible thing Mrs. Canning was about to tell her.

"About your parents."

"Yeah...her parents are murderers," Jack reminded.

"No...her real parents." Abby was stunned. She couldn't believe what Tessa Canning was telling her. "Your mother, she was only seventeen when she had you."

"What about my father?" Abby asked, impatiently.

"He was my brother-in-law," Tessa explained.

"So, Jack and I, we're cousins?" Abby asked still in shock.

"I guess so."

"And you're my aunt?"

"I think so, my dear."

"What great news," Abby cheered as a smile came upon her face. "Is he alive? Where is my mother?"

"They were both killed when you were three."

A frown stretched across Abby's face. "How?"

"A fire," Tessa said softly.

"Where was I?" Abby wondered.

"You were here, actually. Your mother and father had just gotten married that day. They asked me to take care of you for the night."

"Did they marry each other because they had to?"

"No...no...they were young and her parents didn't want her married until she was older."

"Oh...where'd we live?"

"On Main Street. Where you live now actually. After they died, the Cotter's tore down the house and built their store."

"Oh." Abby was confused. She was finding it difficult to understand. "So I'm really Abby Canning?"

"Truly, you are..." Tessa said.

"Why do I live with the Cotter's?" Abby inquired, not wanting to know if they murdered another innocent life.

"You were supposed to live with us, but I was sick. Your grandmother was friends with them. She decided they were a good family to watch you and we were a bad one."

"Oh, I'm sure you would have been a lot better of a parent than both of them put together."

"What should we do, Ma?" Jack asked.

"I don't know." She was such a wise woman, who seemed to run out of solutions. "But go home and act normally. Just do whatever you normally do when you're home. Tomorrow come here and we'll see what we can do. All right, dear?"

Abby gazed at the fire again. "Okay…" She stood up and placed her blanket in the spot where she sat.

"Are you leaving?" Jack speculated.

"Yes. It's time for me to leave." Jack led her to the door and opened it. "Thank you. I'll be here in the morning."

"Bye, Abby."

"Thank you, Jack."

"Bye, Abby!" Mrs. Canning exclaimed just before Abby turned to leave.

"Goodbye, Aunt Tessa," Abby chimed. "I'll see you in the morning." Abby went outside into the pouring rain. She ran to save herself from becoming drenched.

As she approached the Cotter General Store, Abby saw that there were no lights visible in the entire house. *Hopefully no one was awake,* Abby thought. She opened the front door, and tiptoed inside. Abby mounted the creaky stairs and entered her bedroom.

Sleeping with a snore, Abby's pudgy little sister, Constance, tossed and turned in her small bed.

Abby lit a kerosene lantern and dimmed the light very low. She opened her book, *Uncle Tom's Cabin.* The day before, she started reading the book. Abby thought she could relate when the slaves were beaten.

Then she heard patting on her window. She got up from her bed to look out and see what was making the racket.

Abby poked her head outside her bedroom window. "What?" She couldn't see what was below her. She realized it was Nick. "Nick?"

"I've come to take my beautiful girl out," said a voice from below the fog.

"Nick...I'm not your girl."

"Okay, then...I've come to take a beautiful girl out?" he tried a second time.

She looked in her bedroom. "Okay..." Abby dimmed the lamp very low. "Move aside."

"What are you doing?"

"Getting out the only way I can," she explained as one of her legs swung over the side.

"Abby, be careful."

"Don't worry! I'll be fine," she cried out.

Nick was skeptical. Abby closed her eyes and jumped from the second story window. When she was safely on the ground, she climbed to her knees and dusted her skirt off. "So, where are we going tonight?"

Nick was in awe. When he got his grip he said, "I'm leaving tomorrow."

"For Harvard?" They began to walk.

"I'm afraid so."

"Oh, Nick, don't leave."

"I have to. I'm as late as it is."

"Well, I wish you didn't have to go," told Abby.

"Me neither."

"Where are we going?" Abby asked, anxious.

"To a barn party. Some farmer just built a barn down the street. My sister's the son's...well you know. He invited us along."

"Christina has a new beau?"

"No...they've been with each other for months now. He's the father of her baby. That's funny; I thought I had mentioned that to you. I guess not."

"It must've slipped your mind." Abby thought Christina was ridiculous. The rain stopped and the sky was clearing. The stars were popping out and they sparkled and shined as if the rain gave them a bath.

"I have a stagecoach waiting for us at my house," Nick arrogantly explained to Abby.

"That's not very necessary. We're only going to a barn party."

"Well…it's far. I thought it would be nice."

"Yes, Nick, it's fine."

They came upon Nick's house and sure enough, the stagecoach was waiting for them. Abby was a bit insulted. She would have rather walked. The two horses shuffled their feet as they waited for Nick and Abby. Abby hated stagecoach rides. Whenever she knew she had to ride in one, (which wasn't very often,) she took blankets and folded them to place under her.

The man to drive them to the farm wasn't in sight. "Our coachman should be here," Nick was confused.

"I wonder where he is." The coachman came out from behind Nick's house.

"Nature called," he explained.

"Go ahead, Abby, get in," Nick directed. Abby went into the form of transportation and sat down. Nick followed her.

"How far away is it?" Abby questioned.

"Do you know the Keely's?"

"Yes."

"That's the farm we're going to."

"Henry is Christina's beau?" Abby was shocked. Henry was so quiet and shy.

"Yeah…nice kid," Nick smiled.

"Uh-huh."

With one whip from the driver, the two horses were on their way. Abby knew the farm was only a few miles away. Nick was absurd. Then she though she was being crazy. She felt over-worked from learning new things that day.

As the carriage stumbled over rocks, Abby and Nick bounced up and down trying to avoid injuries. "No drinks tonight, Nick."

"None?" Nick seemed disappointed.

"None…I was scared to death when I woke up in the alley. I can't imagine the sort of man that did that to me. I feel filthy and disgusting." Abby shook her head.

"I would have fought him off, Abby. I'm so sorry," Nick sympathized.

She sighed and looked out of the little window to see if they were there yet. The lights from the new barn shone brightly far away. There was a big bonfire and the farm was crowded with friends and family. They heard music and people having a good time.

The stagecoach pulled around the front of the house and came to a sudden halt. The coachman opened the small door and Abby along with Nick came out.

"Finally, we're here!" praised Abby. She straightened her dress.

"I know…it kind of hurts my…"

"Nick!" Christina cut off. "I'm so glad you and…sorry, I forgot your name," Christina said being obnoxious.

Abby rolled her eyes. "Abby…" she reminded, aggravated.

"Oh, yes…Abby, I'm so happy you could come."

"Thank you, Christina. Hello, Henry," Abby greeted.

"Hi, Abby…" he replied.

"You and your father must be very proud and happy the barn is finally finished," Abby tried to start a conversation.

"Yeah…" Henry said. "We wanted it to be done before the winter."

"Well…it's been accomplished."

"It sure has," Christina added. "Poor Henry worked on the barn all by himself, while his lazy father sat on a rock and watched."

"That's not true!" Abby argued. "Mr. Keely is a hard working man, Christina."

"I'm sure he is," Nick agreed. "Let's go to the party." He seemed to be rushing them. Nick led her to the barn where there were people dancing and laughing. Abby loved to see people happy.

One song ended. The band consisted of a guitar, a violin, and a banjo. They started a new song and Nick grabbed Abby's hand to dance. The fire roared in gigantic flames as if were the sun itself lying in the middle of the field. People danced around it and the moment went into slow motion. Expressions on the people's faces brought smiles to others. What a good night it was to end a miserable day.

Tonight was Nick's night to get drunk. He had a few too many beers. He passed out in the barn on stacks of hay. "Would you like to stay in our guest room, Abby?" Mrs. Keely asked with kindness.

"That would be great. Thank you."

"Follow me." Mrs. Keely led Abby to the upstairs of their farmhouse. She opened a door and lit a kerosene lamp.

"You're too kind."

"We haven't seen you in town lately, Abby…Can I tell you a secret?" Abby nodded. "I'm not too thrilled Christina and Henry are getting married." The hefty woman frowned.

"They have plans to marry?"

"Yes…unfortunately. I washed the sheets and blankets for you. I knew some poor girl would end up stranded here because of their beau passing out."

"You are too good, Mrs. Keely."

"Good night, Abby," the farmer's wife said.

"Good night." The older woman closed the door on her way out. Abby looked around. The room was small, but had a big wooden bed. The windows were opened and the curtains swayed in the breeze as if they were ghosts dancing at a ball. She looked out the window and out onto the Keely's land.

They had many acres. The moonlight shone brightly and lit the fields up. No one was at the barn, except Henry and his father cleaning up. Christina was wrong. Both of the Keely men were hard workers. She had no idea what she had been talking about.

Abby thought about her real mother and father. Then she thought about the cruel people she called her parents for so many years. How could they murder someone?

She decided she was tired. Abby took her shoes off and slipped into the big, comfy bed. She fell asleep as soon as her eyelids shut.

"Nick! Nick! Wake up!" Abby whispered loudly as she shook

him.

"Abby…" he said, a bit groggy.

"Yes, it's me. Get up. You're leaving today, remember?"

With his eyes bigger than his nose, he sat up frantically. "For Harvard? Where am I?"

"You're at the Keely's. Now let's go and get you ready." Abby wanted to go see her aunt. She had a bad feeling.

"Just wait…" Nick lied back down squinting.

"We can't wait!" she snapped.

"Why?"

"I need to go." Abby decided to leave. She had no time to waste. "I'll come by before you leave," she said as she ran to the stagecoach. When she reached the carriage, the coachman was sleeping. "Hey!" Abby shouted. "Wake up."

"Sorry, ma'am," he apologized.

"I need to leave," Abby told him.

"I'm so sorry, but I'm not aloud to leave without Nick Porter."

"Well, I am!" she stormed. Abby pushed the man off his seat and decided to drive herself. "How do you work these things?" Abby gave the reigns a little jolt and the horses were well on their way. They sped the dirt roads.

"Whoa!" she halted. When they were in front of Jack's house. Abby ran to the door and knocked on it hard. "Jack! Hello! Anyone home?" she had had enough of this and decided to go in.

Inside, the youngest Canning child was on her knees sobbing. "Katherine? Are you okay? What's wrong?" Abby went to her knees.

"Mama…something's the matter with her."

"What do you mean?"

"She won't wake up!" Katherine was hurting.

"Jack!" Abby stood up on her feet. "Where's Jack?"

"He's trying to wake her."

Abby went to the door Mrs. Canning came out of yesterday and opened it. Jack was in the corner with his head dug into his lap. On the bed, her aunt lay helpless, gray and frail. "Jack…" Abby whispered. He lifted his head. "What's wrong?" she asked with a tear slipping down her soft cheek.

He was in shock. "I think…I think…my ma's…ma's…dead…"

"Don't say that, Jack! Don't!" Abby went into hysteria. "No! Jack! No!"

"It's true…it's true…I tried everything…"

Abby fell to her knees.

"You look handsome, Billy," Liz complemented Billy.

"Do I?" he asked.

"Yes…you are much prepared for that meeting." Liz had to lend some clothes to Billy for the job. He wore a shirt, a fresh pair of trousers, and clean shoes.

Billy sighed. "I'm nervous."

"Don't be. You'll be great."

"I don't know. I've never ridden a horse in my life," he admitted.

"Well…the flyer does say no experience necessary," Liz reminded.

"You're right." Billy stepped outside and felt the cool North breeze riding in from his homeland. A flower fluttered into his hand. The flower looked like the ones that came up every year at his house. The memory of his home made him miss Abby and he wasn't afraid to admit it anymore.

"Are you ready?" Liz interrupted.

"Yes, Liz, I am." Billy took a deep breath. He was uneasy. "Where is it?"

"Down the hill…" Liz pointed to the small river. The night before she had told him it was the Scantic.

"I'll walk you down, Billy, if you'd like?" Liz offered.

"Sure I would…" As they walked down the steep hill, Billy grew more nervous with every heartbeat.

"It's in that building." Liz showed him the big red building, which stood in front of them. Billy started toward the location. "Good luck."

As he entered the building, there were only a few men there. Billy was relieved. He noticed he was overdressed for this occasion. "Name?" a man asked who was sitting at a table. "William…"

The stranger looked up. "Last name?"

"Sanson…" Billy said.

"Well, William…"

Billy hated when people called him William. "Billy, please."

"Billy…can you ride?"

"Nope."

"Can you read?"

"Nope."

"Can you write?"

"Nope."

The man was frustrated. "Can you do anything?"

"Nope…" Billy teased. The man stood up and walked away. "I'm kidding."

The man turned to Billy.

"I'm Calvin Rover. You start Monday," he introduced and shook Billy's hand.

The door stammered as if it were horses on the run. Abby walked to the door to greet the doctor. Doctor Bridge, Sarah's father, was a good doctor. Abby always loved going to his office when she was little; prizes were always the finale of the visit.

"Where is she?" he asked.

"In the bedroom…" Abby responded. Doctor Bridge brushed by her side.

"Abby?" Jack whispered her name so tender. She turned.

"Yes, Jack?" Wiping her tears, Abby's face turned bright red.

"You should go."

"No…" her tone steadied and grew soft. "I…I can't leave you and Katherine alone."

"Abby, I know you have something else to do."

"But it can wait…" she said sternly.

"Jack?" the doctor hollered from inside the bedroom.

Jack rushed to the door. "Go!"

Abby didn't want to make him angry. If leaving were the only way she would make him happy, she would go.

Waiting patiently, Abby hoped Nick would answer the door instead of Christina. "Abby?" Nick opened the door.

"Hello…" she said softly.

"Come in," he rushed. "You look sad."

"Yeah, I am. Jack's mother died this morning."

"I'm so sorry, Abby," he said sympathetic.

"Thanks," she sniffled. "When are you leaving?"

"In an hour or so," he told her.

"Oh, are you feeling okay?"

"Yeah," he chimed. "I have a headache though. I'm sorry about last night."

"It's okay," she lied. Abby had hated yesterday. "Well…" Words did not come to her. She was overflowing with grief. Emotions built up inside her and she was ready to burst.

"I brought your horses back."

"Thank you." He seemed like he was shy.

"What's wrong, Bill…Nick?" she almost slipped.

He sighed. "I'm going to miss you."

"Me too…" Abby hugged him tight and gave him a kiss on the right cheek. "You'll write, won't you?"

"Of course…expect a letter every week."

"You too," she agreed. Nick was empty. He wasn't his normal self.

"Nick…" Christina popped her head from outside. "Your coach is here."

"Thanks, Christina," he said.

"So soon?"

"Yeah…" Abby followed Nick outside.

The cold day made Abby clutch her cloak to her body. The wind howled as if it were a person whistling a tune. "Goodbye, Nick," Christina hugged him. She wiped her eyes.

"Bye, Nick," Abby said as she kissed him farewell.

"Bye." Nick stepped up into the stagecoach.

Abby started to walk away. She sighed. What was there to do? To wait? Wait for what? For Billy to come back? Would he come back?

Abby grasped the lonely moment. It penetrated from inside her body. Her hair danced in the wind, her dress flew freely with the birds, and she walked down the street thinking of nothing.

The sound of the deadly whip slapping her back, muted from her ears. She hated him. She hated her. She hated her parents. Thoughts of why they could be murderers weaved in and out between her two ears. She wanted to say, "I know your secret." But she didn't have the guts to say it. She believed he liked to beat her. It was pleasure to him. When he was through, Abby went to her room and slept.

Abby ripped the bloodstained sheets off of her the next morning. She had to go and see how Jack and Katherine were doing. She stumbled down the stairs, and out the door she went.

People were at Jack's house. Abby didn't know why. She entered their house and found different people all standing around Jack, talking to him.

She found Katherine in her bedroom. She was staring out her window, Abby wasn't sure at what. Maybe it was the grand weeping willows that hung overhead, or the birds in the sky. Maybe she was just looking at the sky, wondering what her mother was doing at the moment in heaven.

"Katherine."

"Yes…" She turned. Katherine was a gentle thirteen-year-old girl. Abby thought she resembled her aunt very much. She was growing into a fine young woman.

"How are you doing?" Abby asked with concern.

Katherine took a deep breath.

"Guess what? I found out we were cousins."

"That's great," she tried to smile.

Abby grinned. "I could still remember thirteen. It seems like yesterday. Life was perfect then. But the past months have changed my life…forever…"

Katherine looked out the window again, and then she turned back to Abby. "Abby, why do you think weeping willows having the name weeping willows?"

Abby had to think for a few moments. "I think…I think they symbolize people's grief. What other tree would be perfect?"

Katherine looked outside again.

"Weeping willows seem to me like the mother tree. It's like if you sit underneath one, its long arms pick you up and bring you to another world."

"Would it bring me to Heaven? To see my mama?" She was so determined.

Abby choked up. "I don't think so…but the willows will listen. They're the best when it comes to listening. They don't talk back."

"Yeah, but…"

Jack opened the door and came into the bedroom. "The funeral's tomorrow."

Abby sighed. "Okay."

"Jack?" a familiar voice came from outside the door.

"In here," Jack replied.

Sarah Bridge, beautiful and kind, had won the heart of Jack. When she entered, she went straight to him and held him. "I'm so sorry…" she whispered in his ear.

They parted. "Tomorrow's the funeral."

"Okay." Sarah looked around. "Hello, Abby. Hello, Katherine."

They both greeted her back. Sarah and Abby had been friends when they were nine. They were never close, but Abby knew they would become better friends because of Sarah and Jack's relationship.

Abby had to dress nice. That day was her aunt's funeral. Black was the color of the day. She told her "parents" where she was going and off she was.

Tessa Canning would be buried in the family cemetery under one of the overhanging weeping willows. They were beautiful.

Abby found Madeline and Thomas Canning, her mother and father's graves. She ran her hand over the top of the gravestone. 1845-1865 was engraved on her mother's and 1844-1865 on her father's.

Every student of Tessa Canning showed up at the ceremony. The windy day allowed petals of different flowers to stream in the air and flow away. The ceremony was radiant. With not a dry eye in the cemetery, everyone remembered who she was.

"She was respected and respectful herself. The kind woman had lived her life to the fullest. This brilliant teacher had lived her life the way she wanted. She wanted to give opportunity to others, and that's exactly what she gave to me," Abby said when it was her turn to speak.

Chapter 9

November 25, 1877

The past month has been different. I've done nothing but play games with Katherine and spend time with her and Jack. Jack and Katherine miss their mother more than you could imagine.

I've had dreams. Bad dreams. About my parents, about Billy. About everything.

The rock has been so lonely and gray. I go there once in a while to read or to clear the dust off the furniture. But every time I go, memories fill my head. I try to put the pieces of the puzzle together. I haven't found where one piece belongs yet. This world is such a mystery. I fear I will never find the answer.

Abby

"Riding horses is hard," Billy told Liz.

"But you've been doing so well," Liz complimented.

They were at the bank of the Scantic River. Liz told him it was her favorite place to go. The cold water pierced Billy's hands as it ran between his fingers.

"Every part of this world is different," Billy discovered.

"If you travel, you will learn there is a very big difference between Connecticut and Vermont." The trees were bare. The leaves no longer rustled in the wind. The branches were cold and lonely.

Billy looked at the sky. It was gray. Snow began to fall gently from the clouds as if feathers were thrown up and fluttered down.

"The first snow of the year is always beautiful," Liz smiled.

Billy agreed. Snowflakes fell onto his face and melted. He felt

Enfield didn't need him. He felt Abby needed him. He wanted to go home. But he couldn't.

"The snow is falling hard," Katherine said. Ever since Abby talked to her that day her mother passed away, Katherine spent time talking to her. They had become practically like sisters.

"Oh, I know," Abby agreed looking out the window.

"It's cold out there," Jack said as he came in with wood to make a fire.

Katherine laughed. "You're covered with snow."

Jack chuckled along with her. He piled the wood and lit it with a match. The fire provided warmth and filled the house.

"Do you celebrate Thanksgiving?" Abby asked. Her family never did and Abby always wanted to.

"Yes, every year," said Katherine. "Does your family?" Abby shook her head. "Why don't you celebrate it with us this year?" she suggested.

"Yes...Sarah's coming," Jack told her. "You should come too."

"That would be nice. Thank you," Abby felt accepted. "Oh my, look outside." The snow twirled, almost as if it were a blizzard. "I'll go home and tell my parents before the storm gets too bad," Abby said.

"Okay..." Jack agreed.

"I'll see you tomorrow to help bake," Abby stood up and put on her cloak. "Bye."

"Bye, Abby," Jack said.

"Bye..." Katherine told her.

Abby went in the snowstorm. It was hard to see, but not impossible. She ran cautiously, being careful of ice. It was now she wished she had a stagecoach.

Abby opened the door and went into her kitchen. Mr. and Mrs. Cotter were at the table. "For Thanksgiving, the Canning's have asked me to go over their house. I'm planning on doing that." Abby wasn't sure what they would say.

"You can't," Charles said.

"We are celebrating it this year," his wife added.

"Why this year?" Abby was careful with her words.

"We want to give thanks this year. That's all."

"You never did before. I've always asked you. You would always say, 'Give thanks I won't be beating you today'."

"This year is different."

"All right." Abby left to go upstairs. She wouldn't stay. For all she knew, they could've made it up on the spot. Maybe they knew she discovered their secret.

"A letter came for you today," Constance handed it over as she left the room.

"Constance?" She stopped in her tracks.

"Did Mother and Father tell you we were going to celebrate Thanksgiving this year?" Abby asked, curiously.

"No...are you ill? They hate the day," Constance told her and then proceeded leaving.

Abby knew it. She jumped on her bed and opened the envelope. It read:

> *My dearest Abby,*
>
> *How are you? I am doing fine. But without you life has been empty, boring. My studies are very hard this year. But with you in my head, you keep me motivated. I want to thank you for that. Tell me how your week has been. I really want to know how the town is doing. I must go. Goodbye.*
>
> *Yours Truly,*
> *Nick*

Abby smiled. It was so nice he cared for the way he did. She wished Billy wrote to her. But he couldn't write. She regretted not teaching him. They could have exchanged letters to one another. It was her own fault.

The wind howled in the sky. The moon tried to peak through the clouds as if it were a child trying to see the window of the baker but can't because the crowd is too overbearing.

Abby climbed underneath her blankets and opened her diary to slip Nick's letter in. The she said Good night to the day.

Abby woke up early the next morning. The moon was still shining and the darkness of the night was still present. She quietly got up and went outside.

There were no footsteps in the snow on Main Street. There was fresh snow topping it. The flurries dusted Abby's hair as she walked to the river. The old canoe was there and she went in it to pole the river.

Old Mann Rock was beautiful when it snowed. She climbed to the top and lay down. Abby closed her eyes and dreamed of Billy next to her, holding her hand. She opened them and saw her side empty. She was lonely. She needed Billy. She needed him to tell her she was beautiful. She needed him to hold her hand.

Her tears froze running down her cheek. She longed for his rough thumb to wipe them away. She longed for him to tell her it would be all right. She longed for everything he gave her. Strength. Freedom. Sunshine. Love. She longed for love.

Abby sat up. The sun was rising. Was Billy watching the sun too? Where he is, maybe it's not the same sun. Maybe he's too far to see it.

She looked up at the rope around the strong arm of the oak tree. She missed swinging on it. They had good memories together.

Abby decided to go to Jack's house. He was always up this early. Sarah, Katherine, and Abby were all going to bake today because tomorrow was Thanksgiving. Abby stood up and jumped down from the rock. She pushed the boat off and hopped inside.

It was beautiful to soar down the river when it snowed. The wind whirled the flakes around. You never knew quite exactly where one would land. That was the beauty of it all.

Abby walked to Jack's house and found Katherine and Sarah already baking. "Hi, Abby," Sarah greeted.

"Good morning," said Katherine.

"Hello. You've already started?"

"We didn't know if you were going to join because of the storm and all," Katherine mentioned.

"I had to make a stop before I came," Abby explained. She put on her apron that she brought from her house. "Where is Jack?"

"He's working," Sarah responded. "Here, Abby, you can make the crust for dessert."

"What are we having?" Abby asked.

"Apple pie," Katherine said, enthusiastically.

"Mmm…apple pie, my favorite."

"Jack's too. Don't tell him, though. It's a surprise," Sarah said.

"I won't." Every hour, the house smelled better and better. The apple pie gave warmth to the house along with the turkey. Abby loved cooking all day. She had never done it before. By the time Jack was home, everything was done. All three women were around the fire. Katherine was reading, Sarah was knitting, and Abby was gazing in the flames, thinking.

"Wow! It sure does smell good in here!" Jack praised. He walked to Sarah and gave her a kiss. "Hello."

"Hi," she smiled.

"I have to go," Abby told everyone. "I'll be here bright and early." She went outside. It was still snowing. She stepped into the deep snow and her feet turned cold that instant.

Abby crept into her bedroom. Constance was still awake. "Where were you?" she asked.

"At the Canning's," Abby explained.

"Oh." She continued writing on a piece of paper.

"What are you writing?"

Constance replied, "A letter."

"Do you have any extra pieces of paper?" Abby asked. Constance handed Abby a piece of paper. Abby wrote:

Dear Nick,

I am great. It's snowing very much here, where you belong. Is it where you are? We have many inches of snow already piled. Tomorrow is Thanksgiving Day. Will you be celebrating? When will you be back? Come home soon. We all miss you. Since I am very tired from the day, I will depart.

Abby

Although Abby didn't feel that way, she wrote it anyway. She never wanted him to come back. She wanted him to stay where he was because there was where he belonged.

Abby dressed in her nightgown, turned off her kerosene lamp, and went to sleep.

It was still snowing, when Abby woke up. The snow was very high, but she still wanted to go.

When she was present downstairs, her "mother" asked her where she was going.

"I am going to the Canning's for Thanksgiving dinner," she replied as she was walking out the door pulling her hood over her head.

"We're having the celebration here."

"But the Canning's have kindly asked me and I just couldn't show up and turn them down," she argued.

"You will stay here...or...your father will take the whip out," she said sternly.

Abby didn't care. She walked out the door as Hattie was entering. "Hattie! Go fetch Abby! Bring her back here!" her mother ordered.

Abby kept walking in the snow. She lost sight of Hattie trying to find her and figured she went back inside.

Taking big steps, Abby couldn't see a thing. She only saw white. She trusted her sense of direction and followed it. Abby tripped. The deep powder covered her, drenching her like the day Billy tipped her over on the boat. She picked herself up and continued to find her way to Jack and Katherine's house.

She finally saw a light and recognized it. It was Jack's neighbor's. She went to the right a little bit and found the door to Jack's house. Instead of knocking, she opened the door and fell inside. Her face, bright red, was as cold as icicles hanging on the house.

"Abby, are you all right?" Sarah rushed toward her.

"I'm sorry," she choked, "I didn't knock."

"It's all right," Sarah assured. "Come on," she led, "sit by the fire."

"Abby, you're here." Katherine came into the room. They gave each other a hug.

"Where's Jack?" she coughed.

"Upstairs...he's getting ready," Katherine explained.

"You both look beautiful," Abby complimented. Sarah had her hair down, with pins holding the sides. Her dress was green and sparkled in the light. Katherine wore a red dress. A velvet one. Black beads gathered her hair.

"So do you," Katherine told Abby. Abby wore a black dress. It was another present for Hattie from her cousin. Her hair was down and nicely curled.

"Thank you."

"Wow, look at these three beautiful ladies I'm having dinner with tonight," Jack said entering the room. "Was it trouble to get here, Abby?"

"My mother did send out Hattie to get me, but I got away. You can't see anything but snow. The wind is treacherous."

"Well I'm glad you are safe," Jack said as he kissed her on the cheek.

"Do you think you'll ever go back?" Liz asked rocking in her chair.

"I suppose one day. Abby will probably be married though, with a house full of children. I'll regret ever leaving and never see her again," Billy replied.

"Don't say that. I am sure she's waiting for you. I bet she's waiting for you at the place you call Old Mann Rock," Liz said.

"I just hope she's all right," Billy shook his head.

"I'm sure she is. The way you talk about her, she's strong. She won't leave you behind."

"I hope you're right."

They spent their day talking. Abby felt strange. She never had a family like this before. They talked about friends, the summer, and of course, Billy. "He'll come back, Abby. I know it," Katherine comforted.

"Thank you."

"Well…" Sarah started, "…I do believe it's time for dinner." They stood up and went to their spots for dinner.

Abby went in the kitchen to fetch the turkey. Sarah followed. "Mmmm…" Jack complimented as Abby carried out the main dish. "It looks delicious."

They all thanked him, said Grace, and began to eat. The table was filled with delight. Jack cut the steaming turkey and the vegetables surrounded the glorious centerpiece.

As they started to finish, Jack began to be quiet. He didn't talk as much as the beginning of dinner. "What's on your mind, Jack?" Sarah asked with kindness.

He shrugged and finished his meal. Sarah saw there was something wrong, but she excused herself to bring them the apple pie.

"Wait…before we eat…" Jack interrupted before everyone started eating dessert. "I have an announcement." Jack stood up, walked to Sarah and knelt down on one knee. He took her hand in his.

"Sarah…my beautiful Sarah…would you be my wife for the rest of my life?" He looked up to her. She began to cry.

Nodding her head, she barely could say yes. They hugged and kissed.

"Ah…now I feel better." Jack was relieved as he sat in his chair. "And don't you worry either. I've taken time to ask your father."

She sighed and reached over to cover his hand with hers. "Thank you."

"How does January first sound to you?" Jack questioned.

"That sounds very nice," she smiled.

For the rest of the night, Sarah couldn't help but stare at her husband-to-be. They were truly in love, anyone could tell.

The night ended wonderful. The storm was still overbearing, so Jack insisted Abby to stay in Katherine's bedroom for the night. She agreed with no regrets.

"Wow, Jack…I didn't see that coming," Abby said. "I just thought you thought the meal was awful. But I'm very glad it was that instead. Congratulations to you both."

They thanked her. As the night grew older, everyone grew tired. But Abby had a question she wanted to ask Jack for a while.

"Do you remember my father?" Abby asked out of the blue.

"Not very well," Jack responded. "I was only five years old. I remember your mother quite well, though. She had your smile. That's what I remember the most. I remember you always needed her. Whenever she put you down, you would cry, so she would have to pick you back up."

Abby chuckled as she gazed into the blazing fire. She could imagine herself like that. She wanted love. She only had love from Billy after they died.

"I wonder…I wonder why Billy's parents were killed," Abby shook her head.

"It's tearing me up inside not knowing. There must've been a good reason," Jack insisted.

"No…knowing my parents," Abby started, "there doesn't have to be a reason."

"I guess you're right," he agreed.

Under the fire's gaze, Katherine fell fast asleep next to Abby. "Wake up," Abby whispered in her ear, "let's go to bed."

Katherine groaned and after a few seconds, drowsily she went to her bedroom. Abby undid her sheets and Katherine climbed into her bed. "Good night," she said.

"Good night," Abby responded. She poked her head out the bedroom door and said Good night to Jack and Sarah, as well.

Abby laid down next to Katherine and felt it was impossible to sleep. She breathed unsteadily. She thought how foolish she was. She was foolish because of Billy. She should have known life was too perfect. Life was too perfect to stay perfect.

Abby closed her eyelids and remembered. She remembered the day he left. It was awful. With Christina and Billy's image in her mind, Abby rolled over to see out the window.

Big snowflakes drove down to the ground a bit more gently. The moon tried to see the white of the nature, but couldn't because the clouds were too greedy to let it.

Abby remembered her kiss, as well. How rare it was. How soft. She wished he was here and couldn't take it any longer. Where was he? Was he okay? Did he ever think of her?

The snow had finally stopped and Billy was glad, too. Riding horses wasn't exactly easy in the deep powder. He was on his way to the meat shop down the road. Liz had asked him to buy some steak for stew she was going to make.

Billy entered the butcher shop. The man behind the counter greeted Billy.

"Why, hello, Billy."

"Hello, Mr. Catterfield," Billy responded.

"What can I do for you today?" Billy handed him a piece of paper. Mr. Catterfield's eyes grew large. "Ah, Liz must be making stew."

"Indeed, she is. Liz makes the best stew I've ever had."

"I agree." He went into the back room to fetch Liz's order. Mr. Catterfield gave Billy the meat and he paid the old man with the money Liz gave him to give the butcher.

"Here you go, Liz," Billy presented. "Here's your meat you wanted. Now I must go to work."

"Thank you, Billy," the gray woman appreciated as she took the beef into her kitchen. "When you come home, hot stew will be waiting."

"I sure hope so…but, I might be back late…I think I'm going out of state tonight."

"All right. Just go, Billy! Or you'll be late!" the woman shooed.

Billy stepped outside and went down the hill to find his orders. He hoped Springfield, Massachusetts was the farthest he was going today because it was cold.

"So, Calvin, where about am I going tonight?" Billy asked as he entered the doorway.

"Greenfield, Massachusetts," he replied without looking at Billy. Calvin Rover was a stern man without a sense of humor. He wore the same pair of trousers with one of the two shirts he owned. His boots were muddy and most of all, a good bath was all he needed.

He pointed to Enfield. "Here we are. Follow the river," he said moving his finger along the map up to Billy's destination. "Greenfield is here."

"Right," Billy said. "I've been there before."

"I want you to wait until George Dilbert gives you a reply." Calvin placed money into Billy's hand. "Here's some money for a hotel tonight."

"All right…where can I find George Dilbert?"

"At the town hall. It's the tallest building in the city. If you get lost, ask. No matter how late it is tonight, give him this letter. Tell him you'll be by to pick it up in the morning."

"Okay." Billy went out the door. He walked out back to the stables to get his horse. Rosie was her name. She was brown with a white spot on her stomach. "Okay, Rosie, are you ready?" Billy questioned, not expecting to hear much of an answer as he climbed on top of her.

Billy motioned Rosie to go to Liz's house. He had to tell her he would not be back tonight.

Inside, he opened the door to a wonderful fragrance. "Liz!" Billy shouted.

"Yes, Billy?"

"I won't be back tonight…"

"Why not?" She came out of her bedroom.

"I need a reply...Calvin gave me money to stay at a hotel."

"Okay," Liz nodded. "Where are you going?"

"Greenfield," Billy told her knowing what she would say.

She gasped. "Are you going to...?"

"No, Liz," he cut her off. "I'm not going back home."

"Why not?"

"It's not my place anymore," he lied.

She knew this wasn't his favorite subject. "Okay...well, be careful...I guess your stew will be lonely."

"Goodbye."

Rosie waited for him under the moonlight, shuffling her feet. "Let's go, girl," he demanded when he straddled her back. With one kick, Rosie trotted to the river.

Memories overflowed his mind as he trotted by the river. The moon shone brightly and made the fresh snow sparkle.

Billy sighed. How much he wished he could read. He was very curious what the letter held.

Greenfield was still the same when Billy arrived. He remembered the bartender scaring him by the Indians. How foolish.

Billy strode in and looked to see the tallest building. He spotted it.

The lights were on, so Billy invited himself in.

"I'd like to speak to George Dilbert, please," he told the woman at the front desk.

"I can take it," she stuck out her hand.

"I'm sorry, I must give this to him personally. I have specific orders to," Billy demanded.

"Okay." The woman stood up and signaled Billy to another room. "Mr. Dilbert, this man is here for you." She left the room.

The dark-browed man looked up from his cluttered work. "Yes, boy?"

"I have a letter for you, sir, from Calvin Rover," Billy handed George Dilbert the letter.

"Ah, yes, I've been waiting."

"Yes, well, Mr. Rover asks for you to respond quickly. I will be here in the morning to pick up your reply."

"Thank you."

"Goodbye, sir."

"Goodbye." Billy left the room and thanked the secretary.

Outside, Billy recognized the town. The tavern was around the corner. He rode Rosie to the building.

Billy knew there was an inn upstairs. Last time, he heard some men talking to each other about it.

Tired and not in the mood for a drink, Billy entered the pub. The cloudy room was fuller than last time he was here. Billy went straight to the counter and asked for a room. He gave the man all his money.

Upstairs, in his room, Billy lit the kerosene lantern. The small room had a tiny bed and a nightstand and that was it. The one window was very small.

Billy uncovered the brown bedcovering and he climbed in.

Abby managed to go back to her house in the deep snow.

When she was inside, she was expecting her "father" to be furious and already have the whip around his hand. Indeed, he was furious, but no whip was in sight.

"Where's your sister?" Charles Cotter asked.

"I don't know…she isn't here?"

"You mean," Cecile was about to break down, "Hattie's lost?"

"What do you mean?" Abby asked.

"Last I saw her was when I sent her out to get you."

"I don't know. I thought she went back in the house."

"Obviously not, Abby. Does it look like it?"

Abby sighed. "I'm sorry."

"My poor girl," her "mother" whined. "She's out there in the cold by herself."

"I'm sure she'll mange. The storm's clearing, she'll be back," Abby explained.

"What if she doesn't?" Abby's "father" suggested. "What if she's dead?"

She thought he was harsh. "Don't worry. I'm sure she can manage one night out there. There are many houses around here. I'm sure one took her in."

"You're right. But if she doesn't come back. You are the reason she is dead," Charles had to say.

Chapter 10

December 16, 1877

*Hello! It has been quite a while since I've written.
I'm so sorry. There's been a lot going on! We are planning
Jack and Sarah's wedding...and Hattie. Poor Hattie. She's
missing. We've asked everyone if they've seen her, but no one
has. The snow stays the same height. One day it melts and
that night, more snow piles on onto it. Oooh...I hope Billy is
safe and settled before the snow ever did hit. I pray every
night for him, as well as Hattie. Even though she isn't my
biological sister, I still have love for her. Hopefully she will
be found safe and will come home. Maybe she ran away. Who
wouldn't want to? Anyway, I just want everything to be the
same. I want to be the same with Billy.*

Abby

"Liz...I'm home!" Billy exclaimed, walking through the doorway.

"Oh, good, Billy," the plumpy woman raced toward him from the kitchen. "I was worried."

"Mmm...It smells good in here," Billy sniffed.

"Well, we've no time to eat," Liz rushed. "There's a boy about your age being hung today for murdering this man. We must go."

Billy's eyes grew large. "Liz, I'm surprised in you! You...you want to see someone killed?"

"He deserves it. That man deserves his head chopped off...slowly!" she rambled as she took his hand and ran out the doorway.

A crowd circled the gallows in the center of town. People threw rocks at the murderer as he sat in a wagon to make his way to the stage for everyone to witness.

"Who did he murder?" Billy was curious.

"The banker. He held him up to get money. Mr. Newbury, that's the teller, refused to give him any money. Jonathan Reed is his name. Funny, he's exactly your age."

Billy was shocked they killed a man this way.

As the boy who Liz named, Jonathan Reed, made his way up the stairs, a man was waiting with a thick noose in his hands. He brought the loop over Jonathan Reeds head as if he were winning a medal.

Jonathan's noose was tightened and he walked toward the middle of the wooden deck. As the fake floor was unlatched, Jonathan Reed fell to his death. Breaking his neck was what happened, Billy figured.

Billy was disgusted. The crowd seemed like it evaporated with only, but a few people left watching the dead, swinging man.

A woman, about Billy's age, stood there crying hysterically. "My poor Jon," she cried. "Why? Why did you do this?" She fell to her knees. "I loved you!"

The only thing that ran through Billy's mind was, it could be Abby.

"Abby!" Katherine shouted.

"Are you okay?" Abby snapped out of her gaze.

"Yes, I am," Abby assured her.

They were sitting on the floor in Katherine's house next to the fire.

"What's wrong? You haven't been the same these last few days," Katherine observed.

Abby sighed.

"I don't know…it's…it's…just something. It's a feeling…I can't explain it," Abby said, very confused. She stood up. "I must go."

"Why?" Katherine's big blue eyes, just stared at her.

"I must…there's something I have to do."

"Would you like me to go with you?"

111

"No, thank you," Abby replied. She proceeded toward the door. "Bye," she said to Katherine as she walked out.

When she was outside, Abby took a deep breath. The day was gorgeous. No clouds filled the deep blue sky. There was only sunshine that heated Abby as if she were an oven.

Abby walked to the river. Something seemed to lure her to the rock. As she climbed into the boat, some kind of movement took over her attention. Down the river was a small boat. She recognized "her parents" inside of it.

Abby knew they were headed toward Old Mann Rock. She decided to walk, instead of going down river by boat. Across the freezing cold river, she went. There was no path. Defeating large obstacles such as fallen down trees and deep snow, Abby made sure to keep quiet.

She reached the glorious rock. Her "parents" climbed it and followed the path toward Billy's house. Abby snuck to his house by the bare forest. Why were they there? What could posses them to come back after eight years? Those went questions in and out of her head as she crouched down to watch what they were going to do.

They entered the house. "All right, Billy!" Abby's "mother" exclaimed, "where are you?"

"We won't kill you," the man whom Abby didn't recognize said.

Charles became impatient. "Come on!"

Abby realized she was being a fool. She was hiding in a bare forest with a bright red dress on. The murderers would be able to spy her.

Abby laid down on the frozen ground. She noticed that they searched the house again. They all met back at the entrance. "Everything's the same," one of the two men said. They exited the house. As the trio stepped down the stairs, Charles Cotter stopped dead in his tracks looking straight in Abby's way.

I'm seen, I'm seen, she cried in her head.

"What is it, Charles?" her "mother" asked.

Charles looked away. "Nothing…I thought I saw something."

They continued toward the river. Abby couldn't bear to look as they passed her. She took a deep breath when they were no longer in sight.

"Abby," she told herself. "You must stop getting almost caught." She stood up and went inside Billy's house.

Abby walked around to see if they left anything because they would be back for it. She found nothing out of the ordinary. She went into the library. Every time Abby visited, she would read from Billy's father's journal. She was nearly done. The tiny journal educated her about the bloody Civil War: No one would believe the fear the soldiers had, the feeling at the battlefield, or the taste of victory they had when it was all over with.

He missed his son and wife. Gregory was nearly killed being shot in the arm. The infection spread quickly. Word would've never reached his wife seeing no one knew where they lived. It was obvious he must have loved his son. In fact, it was certain. This man's love was greater than the universe. It was greater than anything that ever existed.

Abby looked out the window. It was night. The snow came down heavy, piling onto the old powder. She wouldn't go home. She would stay the night. She was too scared to go through the woods alone.

Abby went into the parlor. Firewood was already near the fireplace. She had known this would occur one night. Billy was the one that taught her to build a fire. "Air...air...and air... " he always said. "Those are three things a fire always needs."

She was lucky he had taught her how. She would be cold and miserable that night. Abby lit the kerosene lantern and fetched blankets from Billy's bed. She lay near the fire and just stared at the ceiling. Abby thought about Christmas. *A Christmas without Billy? What kind of Christmas was that? It's no way to celebrate.*

She did qualify to receive his gift. She wondered what it could possibly be. Abby thought of the murderers. *What if they damaged his miraculous gift?*

No one knew where she was. Everyone except for God. God, the one man whom helped her get through these times. He knew what she was feeling and thinking. He knew Billy's emotions and thoughts too.

God knew everything.

Abby decided to read. She walked into the dark library. She searched the shelves for a book to read. Abby returned to her spot by the fire with the book and water she had pumped earlier.

She read. Her eyes were tired, her head confused with different things. Reading was her favorite thing to do. No matter what was happening, she always had time to read. It cleared her head; gave her peace.

Abby enjoyed this old English book. A new sense of style. A new sense of imagination.

William Shakespeare, she thought, *was a magical writer. He touched his audience with only words.* He was a man she admired.

Billy was on his way. Calvin Rover gave him orders to go down to Hartford, Connecticut. It wasn't far, but he enjoyed coming home.

He decided to stop and rest. He halted Rosie and tied her reigns around a tree. As he began to sit down, he heard a distant noise.

"Hello?" He looked around. "Anyone here?"

A scream from a woman came from the forest. Billy ran to see what was happening. As he approached the scene, he saw a woman being tormented by a man. She struggled to get free.

"Help me!" she screamed. "Please!"

Billy ran toward them. He pulled the raging man off her. "Get off her!" Billy shouted.

"Hey!" the man yelled back. "Stay out of this!"

Billy resisted him to go back on her. "Go!" he ordered her. She crawled away, whimpering.

The man took a swing at Billy. He missed. Billy punched him in the face, sending him off his feet. "Run! Toward the river!" Billy kicked the man. He punched him until his nose bled, heavily.

"He'll be knocked out for some time," Billy told the woman. They sat at the bank of the river. She had black and blue eyes and her hair was matted.

She wiped her hair from her face. "Thank you."

"Billy," he said.

"I'm Gloria," she introduced.

"Who was that?" Billy was curious.

"My boyfriend...actually now, not my boyfriend anymore. We ran away to be married. He got drunk and decided to go crazy on me," Gloria explained.

"Where were you headed?"

"Windsor," she told Billy. "He has family there."

"Where are you going now?"

"I really don't know," she shook her head.

"Come to Enfield. There are really nice people there."

"Well, we should get going before he gets up."

"I think so," she agreed as Billy helped her up. "So why were you in these parts of Connecticut, Billy?"

"Business," he explained as he gave her a boost up on the horse.

"Liz?" Billy called as he swung the door open. Liz came out from the kitchen.

"Billy, you're home."

"Yes...I've brought someone."

Gloria walked into the house. Her curly blonde hair shined in the sun. Her calico dress was filled with soot and a few rips here and there.

"Oh, Billy." Liz hugged Gloria. "Abby is beautiful."

"Um..." he tried to correct.

"Why didn't you tell me? I would've made a special dinner. Oh, dear, he's talked about you an awful lot."

Gloria looked at Billy surprised. "You have?"

"No," Billy said. "Liz, this is not Abby. This is Gloria."

"Oh?" Liz blushed.

"Yes," he replied.

"I'm so sorry, Gloria. I had no idea." Liz looked at Billy. "I have some questions for you young man."

"Yes," Gloria announced. "Let's start with this one. Who is Abby?"

Abby woke up with the snow still coming down. She reloaded the fireplace with more logs of wood. Then she went into Billy's basement. She found beets. And beets were what she ate for breakfast.

She read more of "Romeo and Juliet." *The love they had for each other was so real*, she thought. She decided to put the book down and go to Gregory Sanson's journal:

Journal,
Abraham Lincoln, our president, has been shot today. This war is finally over, but the man who wanted to see it truly happen has now been murdered.

I will return to my dearest wife and my son, Billy. Four years I haven't seen them. My Billy is five years now. He will look different. My Elizabeth, she will be twenty-one.   I hope our home has not changed. I hope the rock still stands. I hope life will be great, once again.

Journal,
I am one day away from the rock. I hope to get there before sunset. I must go now.

They all sat by the fire. Liz gave Gloria and Billy some tea. Billy told Gloria the long story about Abby. She was very interested.

"Why did you leave?" Gloria asked, reminding Billy of Abby.

"I've already told you. The murderers have come back," Billy was frustrated.

"Oh…and do you know why they came back after eight years?" she questioned.

"I don't know," he lied.

She found it! After reading for quite some time, Abby finally revealed why they were murdered. The passage read:
Journal,
I am in quite a state of shock. Elizabeth and I, we were going to

buy the Cotter General Store. Mr. Charles Cotter was being evicted and thrown in jail because I caught him cheating and stealing.

One day, he was paying some man to kill a man named Johnson Habor. Luckily, I caught him before Mr. Habor was killed and I reported him.

His wife took him out of jail. Now, I'm afraid, he's after me because I have turned him in.

That was the last page. Gregory and Elizabeth Sanson died because they were innocent people and wanted the world to be good. Abby couldn't stand it. She was ashamed to have called the Cotters her family all these years.

She stood up and went to get water for the fire. Abby poured it over the hot coals, took her cloak, and ran out the door.

Abby raged through Main Street. She was mad at the world; mad at God. Deciding to confess it in the church was hard. Outside the church doors were men. They were handing out flyers. "Have you seen him?" one man pleaded. "We must put him to justice."

Abby took one and barged through the church doors. Inside, she knelt down in a pew and bowed her head. "Oh, my dear God," she said in her head, "please forgive me, for I have sinned. I am mad at you for giving me such bad news!" She recited the *"Our Father"* and felt better.

As she walked outside, she looked at the flyer to find out why these men were raving about justice. She found the impossible that made her life turn to the worse. Billy's face sketched on the flyer was centered in the middle. It read:

WANTED DEAD OR ALIVE
BILLY SANSON
$1,000 REWARD

Abby couldn't believe her eyes. He had lied to her. He left because he murdered a man, in which he himself, thought was intolerable.

She broke down and burst into tears. The men who distributed the papers rushed to Abby.

"Are you all right, ma'am?" one of them asked. She could only lie down, in the middle of the street and grieve, for her heart was broken.

She was brought to Jack's house. Abby lay in Katherine's bed, her face reddened from sobbing. She woke up from her little nap. "Jack?" she pouted.

"No, Abby," Sarah's kind voice replied, "it's me, Sarah."

She sighed. "Oh." Sarah helped her to sit up. "Where's Jack?" she wondered aloud. "I need to talk to him."

"I'll go get him," Sarah told her, leaving the bedroom.

Moments later Jack walked in, alone. "Abby?" he whispered.

"Oh, Jack...I know," she cried.

"Know what?"

"I know..."

"Abby, not again. You're just going through a memory relapse. You already know who murdered Billy's parents." Jack patted her shoulder. "Now, lay down and go to sleep."

She couldn't look at him. "Jack!" she shouted. "Listen to me! I know about Billy and why he left. I know why Mr. and Mrs. Sanson died and the scariest part of all, I know why the murderers keep coming back," she babbled.

Jack looked at her in disbelief, not sure if he wanted to know why. "He murdered a man, Jack. Probably one of the murderers. Actually, I'm sure of it."

"Are you..."

"Positive!" Abby saw his expressions. Jacks face was tense and looked ashamed.

"I can't believe it."

Abby closed her eyes and let a tear free.

"You know what hurts the most? He lied to me about it all. I bet he knew my parents were the murderers. He lied."

"And hurting you he didn't want to do. Wasn't him leaving hard enough?" Abby nodded. "He probably knew you would find out," Jack said.

"I'm still mad," she sternly chattered.

"Me too, Abby...we don't know the story yet."

"Right. Promise to not tell anyone?"

"I won't," Jack promised.

December 20, 1877

Dear Diary,

Hello. I am indeed very angry at this moment. Liars and more liars have entered my life. I thought I could trust Billy, but that was one big LIE!

Anyway, four days until Christmas Eve and five until the day. The town is having a party. I don't plan on attending. I'd rather stay home. Besides, whom would I go with?

I must go now. Constance is coming.

Abby

"Abby?" Constance's high voice came from around the corner.

"Yes, Constance? What is it?"

Abby could hear the faint noise of Constance's whimper. As she turned the corner, the red and swelling of Constance's face was revealed.

Abby ran to her. "What happened?" she asked.

"Daddy...he's...beat my face!" Constance cried.

"Oh, what for?" Abby questioned, with sympathy.

"He said he wanted Hattie back!"

"Oh, come on," Abby led her younger sister to her cot. "Lie in bed. He has no right to do that to you."

"Doesn't he do that to you?" Constance sobbed as she pulled her blankets over her face.

"Yes, but, see...I'm not...his daughter."

"What?" Constance's curls bounced.

"I'm not your sister," Abby whispered.

Constance couldn't help but burst into tears. "Ah…it's okay, Constance. Don't worry. Everything's going to be all right," Abby assured her mind as she stroked Constance's hair.

"How can you say that?" Constance whispered. "How can you be so sure?"

Abby couldn't help but shrug her shoulders and shake her head. "I don't."

The next dinner in the Cotter household was silent. A word hadn't existed. "A letter came for you today, Abby," Charles said.

Abby looked at him wide-eyed. "A letter?"

"Yes, a letter! Isn't that what your father said?" her "mother" snapped.

"Uh…um…yes," Abby stuttered. "From whom?"

Charles looked at her as if she had three heads. "Sorry," she apologized as she looked down to her empty plate. She had eaten everything. And she was still hungry.

After Abby helped clean up, her "father" gave her the letter.

She knew it was from Nick. He hadn't written to her in two weeks. Abby ripped the envelope open and it read:

My dearest Abby,

I am so very sorry I haven't written to you in a while. I've been quite busy with my studies. On top of that, there has been something I had to think about. With all the stars in the sky, I wouldn't want any other than you. Abby, you're what I think about in the morning when I wake and what I think about before I go to sleep at night. There's no other way to put this, but: I love you. I hope you don't take me as forward, but it's true. I don't want to write to you anymore. I want to wake up next to you in the morning. Oh, dear Abby, will you marry me?

Love Always,
Nick
P.S. I've talked to your father. He said it would be
fine.

Abby couldn't believe what she was reading. She could only sit on her bed in awe and look at the letter, reading it over and over again. *She was actually proposed to! What a feeling!* she thought.

As the sun set on the world, Abby thought and thought; *what to do?* She thought about Billy. She felt anger and shame, as well as the hole in her heart. Perhaps if she married Nick, that hole would fill up.

Love was something she lacked for Nick. And pride was what she now lacked for Billy. Abby gathered a piece of paper and an instrument to write with. She wrote:

Dear Nick,

Hello.

Abby was wordless. What else could she possibly write? Besides her mind wasn't made up yet. She proceeded:

My future. I don't know where to begin. My life will change forever, as well as others. Nick, I know you know about Billy. He currently is out of town. I don't know where. I know you haven't liked Billy. I can't imagine why because he is kind and been a great friend to me. But also, I am very ashamed of him because of past experiences. I needed to tell you. I needed to tell you there will always be a feeling inside me that will always love him. But, I love you, too. And I will take your proposal. I will marry you.

Love,
Abby

Chapter 11

December 21, 1877

Dear Diary,

> *Yesterday, I think I made the worse possible choice in my life. I have agreed to marry Nick Porter.*
> *Last night, I lay awake, wide-eyed and hoping Billy would come. I hoped my life was all a big nightmare. Could it be?*

> *Love,*
> *Abby*

Abby stood up straight in front of her mirror. She combed her hair and it was long. Very long. She thought she should cut it. She knew it was a bad idea.

Abby was on her way to Jack's house. She was going to tell him the dreadful news. She knew he wouldn't be pleased. But it was all for the best. Right?

Jack answered her knock. He greeted her and invited her in. Sarah sat in a rocking chair in front of the fire. "Hello, Abby."

"Hi," Abby smiled. "Jack, I came here for a reason."

"You did? You just didn't want to scc us?"

Abby chuckled. "Of course I did. Well, I don't know why I am so nervous. But you're like a big brother to me and it wouldn't be right not to tell you."

"What is it, Abby?"

"I'm getting married," she finally blurted out.

Sarah gasped. "Congratulations, Abby. I'm so happy for you."

"Thank you," she said. Abby saw her cousin's face turn into a frown.

"To whom?" he demanded.

Abby paused.

His voice became much louder. "Abby, to whom?"

"Nick Porter," she whispered. Jack rose up to his feet from where he sat as if he were a bullet. "Jack! Calm down! Please! I'll take care of myself. I promise!"

"Abby, you're making a big mistake," he told her straight out, calmly. "I know you. I know you still dream about Billy. I know you can't take him out of your mind. I know he's what you think about every second of the day."

Abby began to cry. He knew her so well. "I'll be leaving in two weeks. Don't worry, I'll be here for your wedding." Abby walked out the door.

As Billy walked the streets of Enfield, he wondered if Abby could wait until Christmas Day for her gift. He wondered if that jerk people called Nick was still around.

Wondering was bad.

It was four days before Christmas Day and Billy still hadn't had a present for Liz. So, with some money he earned from spending many hours on horseback, Billy was out to buy Liz something.

He knew there was a silversmith in town, and Billy wanted to buy Liz a nice locket.

Inside the shop, there was an older man and a boy about thirteen years old by his side. Billy knew that the boy must've been Mr. O'Layer's apprentice.

"How do you do?" Mr. O'Layer kindly asked Billy with his Irish accent. Mr. O'Layer was an immigrant from Ireland. He had come with is wife and baby girl. It was easy to see they were very poor. He wore the same trousers and dirty red shirt everyday. His beard was long, but went along with his bushy brows. They looked like they were two napping caterpillars above his blue eyes.

"I need a special order, Mr. O'Layer."

"What would that be?"

Billy told him his idea for a gift for Liz. She had been so nice to him, he wanted to get her something special.

Dear Abby,

Could you get yourself a wedding gown? I know Miss Parson's has a nice selection. Just tell her when I return, I will pay. I want you to look ravishing. I know you will. While you're there, ask her for some everyday dresses as well.

Love you always,
Nick

Abby dreaded this choice. But while she was at it, spending Nick's money would be nice. Miss Parson's shop was on Main Street down by the river. Abby walked to her little shop entitled, "Parson Gowns."

Abby entered the small shop. Miss Parson sat behind her desk with her head down, fumbling with papers. She looked up as Abby came through the door. The young dressmaker smiled as Abby came up to her desk. Amelia Parson was her name. She always wore the best clothing in all of the town. Abby knew she wasn't much older than herself, but Amelia did take over her mother's place in the business when she passed away. Everyone had to admit, "Parson Gowns" was doing much better in the last year than the past years when her mother ran the shop.

"Hello, Abby, can I help you?" she greeted.

"Of course. I am going to be married to Nick Porter in two weeks and I need a wedding gown suitable for the occasion."

"Ah, Mr. Porter. I've heard he had his eye on you."

"You have?" Abby sounded surprise.

Amelia Parson nodded her head. "Well, let's go in the back. I have some wedding dresses already made, but if you don't like the styles, I would be more than happy to make one for you."

Abby and Amelia went in the back room. There were magnificent gowns all hung up and never worn. Abby admired them all.

"I adore them all, Miss Parson."

"Well, we can try them all. Sometimes when they're on, you change your mind."

So, Abby tried on all the white gowns. One after the other. She finally chose one. It was made of silk and lace. The lace grasped her neck with a gold broche centering it. The skirt puffed out. It made Abby feel as if she were wealthy.

She felt important.

"This is the one!" exclaimed Abby.

"Oh, Abby, you're going to make a beautiful wife."

Abby smiled. "Thank you."

"Is there anything else on your wish list?" Amelia Parson asked.

"Actually there is. Nick wanted me to buy dresses. I'm not sure my wardrobe would exactly be fit for Boston."

"Oh, I agree. If you're going to marry a man like Nick, you need to have beautiful clothing as well. Day or evening?"

"Both. Could we try some party dresses as well?"

Miss Parson nodded. "Of course."

Abby returned to her bedroom just before sunset. She couldn't wait for her new wardrobe to be ready.

She looked out her window; snow began to fall. Light, gentle snowflakes fell as if they were ashes from a fire in Heaven. But a fire in Heaven? Heaven had no such things.

Billy entered Mr. O'Layer's shop. He told him Liz's gift would be ready and Billy trusted he was right.

"Ah, hello, Billy," Mr. O'Layer greeted.

Billy nodded. "Mr. O'Layer."

The silversmith went into another room and came out with a gift Liz would admire forever. He thanked, paid, and said goodbye to Mr. O'Layer. It was near dark, so he needed to get home.

Billy opened the front door to see Liz knitting. "Hello, Billy."
"Hi."
"What do you have in your hand?"
"Oh, nothing. Just a gift," he teased.
"For who?"
"You."
Liz's eyes lit up. "Oh, Billy…"
Billy shook his finger at her. "Ah, ah, ah, Liz, two days until Christmas."
"But…"
"Nope." Billy went into his corner where he slept and slid Liz's Christmas present under his cot.

"Oh, Billy, Calvin came hear looking for you earlier. He said he had a job for you," Liz informed.

"Okay, I'll go." He kissed her cheek. "I'll be right back."

Calvin Rover, was as usual, sitting at his table looking frustrated upon mounds of papers. He looked up and seemed startled as Billy came through the door. "Billy."

"Yeah?" Billy answered.

"I got yourself a job."

"For what? Where?"

"Tomorrow."

Billy rolled his eyes. *Tomorrow?* he thought. Tomorrow was Christmas Eve.

"Excuse me, boss," Frank Newton cut in.

"What is it, Frank?" Calvin seemed bothered.

"Look," Frank chuckled, "Charles Cotter has himself a missing daughter." Frank Newton pointed to the newspaper.

Calvin grinned. "That old con. He deserves it."

Billy's eyes grew large. "It ain't funny!" he shouted.

"What ain't, Sanson?" Frank frowned. "This man almost put us out of business."

Billy raced the wind out the door.

"Liz? Liz?" Billy hollered as he walked up to the house.

Inside, Liz looked frightened from Billy's cry.

"What is it, Billy?"

"Abby...I think she's missing," Billy panted.

"Your Abby?"

"Yes. I have to go!" He looked around the house frantically. "But before I go." Billy stumbled to his cot and slipped her gift from under the cot. "I want to give it to you now."

Billy presented Liz with her silver locket. Liz, wide-eyed, cupped it into her frail hands. "I had your name engraved onto it."

"Thank you."

"Open it!" he said anxiously.

Liz opened the small heart carefully. Inside, was a picture of her son on one side of the locket he had found. On the other side, a picture of her husband, just before he went to war. Liz's tears rolled down her pale cheeks. "Oh, Billy, it's beautiful. I'm going to miss you."

"Me too, Liz. But I really have to go."

"Okay. You need your present too." Liz went into her bedroom and brought out a pair of wool trousers and a knitted sweater. "Put these on so you're warm."

"Thank you." Billy slipped on his new attire and hugged Liz.

"Bye, boy."

"Bye, Liz. Thank you so much...for everything."

"No...thank you." Billy shut the door behind him as he went out the door to fetch Rosie.

It was a bit passed dawn of Christmas Eve. He had followed the river all the way up the states, passing spectral towns in the night.

He thought of a poem Abby once read him. It was about Paul Revere. He felt like Revere riding on horseback to tell the towns the British were coming.

Listen my children, and you shall hear,
Of the midnight ride of Paul Revere.

Those were the lines he remembered. Abby had to memorize the entire poem for school. He remembered her being very proud of herself when she had the poem right.

Billy sighed. He decided to rest for a little while. Clean water is what he longed for. Clean water was what he didn't have, either.

The day was old. With all but a few thin clouds, the sky was absolutely blue. *What a beautiful Christmas Eve it was,* Billy thought. After he rested a while, Billy climbed Rosie and started toward Abby.

Abby rowed down the river. She was headed for Old Mann Rock. As she went closer, she realized how she had forgotten how much Old Mann Rock looked like Heaven during Christmas.

Abby meandered upstairs to Billy's bedroom. The room was the same as she left it. She was lying down in Billy's small bed, when she thought of how much she resented Nick. She couldn't believe she had accepted his proposal. Maybe it was because she wanted to escape from this life. But a life without waiting for Billy? How could it be possible? She couldn't imagine it.

Mr. and Mrs. Nicholas Porter.

Abby rolled onto her stomach and dug her head into the bed. It was strange. To take out her bad thoughts, she went downstairs to make a fire.

Billy had reached the town a few hours after dusk. He was overflowed with joy. The town had been the same. Men were coming in and out of Spring's Tavern and lanterns shone their mischievous glow from the ships that slept peacefully on the water.

The waterfront sparkled and Billy felt happy for the first time. He was home.

Billy set aside his happiness for a while and followed the smaller river to Old Mann Rock, being cautious to not be spotted.

Abby lay on the sofa with a wool blanket thrown onto her. She had pulled a random book out of the library. As she read, the flames of the fire danced with each other as if they knew the surprise which was awaiting for Abby.

Billy saw the old canoe he gave to Abby docked on the riverbank. That meant Abby was there. He couldn't help but take a deep breath. Billy climbed to the front door. He took another deep breath. He grasped the doorknob.

Abby had heard something. She whipped the blanket off of her and stood to see the front door. As the door slowly opened, Abby saw those familiar eyes she loved.

Could it be?

She just awed over the fact that the person opening the door…was Billy. He closed the door behind him and looked at Abby. She looked more radiant than ever.

Abby looked away to hide her tears from him. "Abby, it's okay," he told her.

She walked over to him and hugged him. Abby sobbed as she held him for the first time in, what seemed to be…forever. "I can't believe you're back. I really can't."

"Me neither," Billy said as he held her tighter. He looked out the window. Snow began to fall. It truly was a magical night.

Billy and Abby sat in front of the fire talking about what happened when Billy was away. He told her about Liz and how kind she was to open her home to him.

Abby told Billy that Jack's mother passed away and about Sarah and Jack's engagement. She fell asleep lying in front of the fire. Billy, lying next to her, watched her sleep. She was so peaceful. He couldn't help but think that it was truly good to be home.

It had been a mistake. Leaving her the way he did. With her beating mother and father. With Nick. Then he remembered, she hadn't mentioned Nick. But that was quite fine.

Abby opened an eye and caught Billy gazing at her. She smiled. "I thought it was a dream; that you were home," she whispered.

"No, I'm here. I'll never leave again. I promise." Abby knew he meant it. Saying goodbye to one another was way too hard to do it again.

"The murderers, they came."

"They did?" he asked, shocked. "Did they see you?"

"No, I hid. I know they're my parents."

Billy gasped. "I had no idea."

"You didn't?"

"No. I'm telling the truth."

"I'm sorry." A tear slammed down her cheek.

"For what?" She couldn't speak.

"Oh, Abby, it's not your fault. They're totally different people."

"They're not my parents."

News. News. News. Everything just hit him at once. "No?"

"No. Jack's my cousin."

"Good news?"

"Yes, very good."

Abby seemed, confused. As if she couldn't believe what she was saying. "I have missed you so much. You don't even know."

"Oh, but I do. I've missed you the same," Billy reminded her.

Abby rolled to her stomach to gaze at the fire. "Did you like Enfield? That's where you were, wasn't it?"

"Sure, I did. Not as much as here, though."

"But you did like being with people?"

He nodded. "It was so nice. Sometimes I missed being alone, though."

"I can imagine."

Christmas morning, Abby woke up to her side empty. "Billy?" Abby searched. "Where are you?"

Billy came into the kitchen just before Abby entered the room. "Water? What for?" She observed his pail he handled.

"Ice. Since I'm back, I've got to get settled."

"I see." Abby pulled up a chair for her at the kitchen table. "Billy, I am just dying inside."

He smirked knowing why. "But why?"

"My Christmas gift," she called out.

"I knew it. You haven't changed," he said, setting the pail down.

"But, Billy, I've waited so long and…"

"Say no more. Come on," he led her to his parents' bedroom.

"Close your eyes," he teased as they reached the door.

"All right." Abby shut them both tight.

Billy opened the door and the chair was easily in sight. "Okay. You can open them now."

Abby opened her eyes. For standing before her was a rocking chair. "Oh, Billy," she gasped, "it's lovely."

The beautiful chair was made out of maple wood, along with designs and carvings engraved into it. "I knew you would like it. I have made you a chair so we could sit together at night now by the fire."

"I love it." She hugged him. "Thank you so much, but how could we rock together when I'm the only one who has one?"

"Ah, my dear Abigail, for I was one step ahead of you."

Her eyes lit up and she chuckled. "You were?"

"My chair is in the corner over there," he pointed out.

Abby laughed. "You're great."

They gradually went downstairs with each of their chairs in their arms.

"I'm sorry, Billy, I lack a gift for you."

"Don't you know? You're all I need."

"I'm being serious…"

"No…I'm serious! You are, Abby. Don't ever change."

"I'll try not to."

"Shall we try?" Billy suggested after placing his rocker next to Abby's.

"Sure."

They both sat on their chairs.

"Heaven!" Abby praised.

After they rested in their chair for an hour, Billy and Abby walked to the rock.

It was a beautiful Christmas Day. Blue skies all around them. Birds singing their songs. Things seemed to be back to normal.

"So, your sister is missing?"

Abby nodded.

"That's the reason I came back. I thought you were."

"I wish you didn't," Abby sorrowfully told him.

Billy frowned. "Why not?"

Abby looked down. "Because I have to leave."

"What do you mean? You're going to stay here with me."

She shook her head, sniffling. "I'm getting married."

He didn't understand. "What are you talking about? To who?"

"Nick Porter," she whispered, looking up at him. His face was in shock. Blank. Not knowing what emotion to show. "I'm sorry. I didn't know you were coming back. I wanted to start a new life."

"Do you love him?"

Abby couldn't speak.

"Do you?"

"I'm leaving in two weeks for Boston."

"You're leaving?" Billy raged.

"Yes," she whimpered.

"But, Abby, do you love him?"

She shook her head. "No," she said softly.

"Then why?"

"Because we can't be together."

Chapter 12

December 25, 1877

Dear Diary,

> *A lot has happened. I have no time to speak. I will tell you later.*
>> *Abby*

"Why, Abby? Why can't we be together?" Billy's tone was hurtful. She looked down once more. The words wouldn't come out. "Tell me. I'll fix it."

"Because…because you've murdered a man. Did you think I'd never find out?"

"I…"

"For God's sake, Billy, you're wanted! There are posters with your name on them."

"But nobody knows where I am. Nobody knows where my home is."

"Oh, but my parents do. They'll tell the police. To get what they want; they'll do anything." Abby looked out in the horizon.

"I'm sorry," he apologized

"I just want to know why."

"Well, one night they came. I didn't know they were your parents. There were four of them. I wanted them to leave because I knew they were the ones who murdered my parents. I remembered their tone of voice. And I thought if I killed them, then they wouldn't come back. We would live the way we wanted to.

"So, I took the rifle from the kitchen, and shot it from a distance. I hit a man and he went down. The rest of them fled with him and warned me they would be back."

Abby shook her head slowly. "I was so happy. But then I thought they would come back for revenge. I had to leave."

"I can't believe what you're saying, Billy." She stood up. "You were glad you killed someone?" She gave Billy a glare as if she despised him. "I've got to go."

Abby ran into the woods hoping Billy would follow her.

But he didn't.

Abby knocked on Jack's door, panting. Sarah answered. "Hello, Abby," she smiled. "Come in." Abby greeted her cousin's bride-to-be and went inside.

"Merry Christmas," Katherine said as she entered the room.

"And a Merry Christmas to you," Abby replied. "Is Jack home?" Abby asked Sarah.

Sarah nodded. "He's getting dressed. He'll be right out."

"What are you doing for Christmas today?" Abby wondered, making conversation.

"We're going to my father's for Christmas dinner," Sarah told her.

"Oh. Sounds fun."

Jack entered the room, a bit surprised Abby was there.

"Hi, Jack. I just wanted to let you know Billy is home."

"Thank you," he said sternly.

"Oh, Abby," Sarah mentioned as if she had almost forgotten. "Will you do the honor of being my maid-of-honor?"

Abby smiled gratefully. "I would love to."

"Could you come by tomorrow so we could go to Parson Gowns to get a wedding gown?"

"Sure. Well, I just had to stop by, so I must be going now." Abby turned to leave.

"Merry Christmas, Abby," Jack said.

"Merry Christmas," Abby replied as she turned and smiled at her cousin. And then she was out the door.

"I have to make an errand," Jack spoke when Abby was gone. He put on his coat and he left the same way Abby had.

Why did she leave? Why was she even more stubborn than before he had left? Billy was walking back to his house. Why didn't he run after her? He couldn't. It was too risky being seen in town.

No wonder she left. He was being selfish. What did it matter? All that mattered was her and nothing else, but her.

"Billy!" a distant voice shouted which seemed to be from the river.

It was Jack.

"Over here, Jack!"

They met halfway and then started toward the porch. "Good to see you, my friend," Jack smiled.

"How did you know where I was?" Billy asked.

"Abby." Jack looked out in the woods. "I'm real worried about her."

"I know. Why is she marrying him?"

"Don't know. But I think she'll change her mind. As stubborn as she is, she can soften up a bit."

"I know you tried your best. Watching over her, I mean."

"Yeah. Especially when she was raped. I still feel guilty."

Billy frowned and looked at his friend. "Raped?"

Jack met his glare. "You don't know? She didn't tell you?"

"No." Billy shook his head.

"The night Nick got her drunk." Jack rolled his eyes. "I reckon it was him. She woke up in the alleyway, bare."

"Poor Abby. Why? Why does she have to marry this bastard?" Billy was furious, but calm at the same time.

"I have to start back home soon, but I wanted to ask you something."

"Anything."

"Be by my side when I'm married?" Jack inquired.

"I would love to, but I don't know if you know, I'm wanted in this town."

"Abby told me. Don't worry. It'll be a small wedding. No sheriffs or anything."

"Abby's parents won't be there?"

Jack shook his head. "Nope."

"All right then," Billy agreed.

"I'll be over in two days with your wardrobe. Sarah demands these clothes," Jack chimed.

Billy laughed at the remark.

Abby woke up the next day; more excited about Sarah's wedding gown than she was about her own. As Abby was getting ready, she felt bad leaving Billy. After all, he did risk a lot coming here.

She walked Main Street, cold. Though she had her cloak on, the wind went through and she felt as if a thousand icicles were going through her body. Abby was supposed to meet Sarah at the shop around ten o'clock. She figured she was late because Sarah was already there.

"I guess I am late," Abby announced as she passed through the doorway.

"No…I was just early," Sarah told her looking around the room at the fine stitches.

Amelia came in from the other room smiling at Abby's presents. "Hello, Abby. Are you here to pick up your dresses?"

"No," Abby replied. "I'm just here to help Sarah."

"Abby, you came here to get a dress?"

"I did. Actually, I had a large order."

"Indeed," Amelia agreed. "Your gown isn't quite ready yet, but if…"

"Don't be silly. I am not leaving for another two weeks," Abby reassured the dressmaker.

"All right then. Sarah, would you like to go in the back with me to pick your selection?"

"Of course," Sarah said with no regrets.

Abby wished she was this excited when she had come to shop for her gown. "Abby? Are you coming?" Sarah asked, following Ms. Parson in the back.

"I'll be there in a minute," Abby told her.

She went outside to see the wanted poster of Billy she had only glanced at on the way in. The sign was the same one she had seen at the church. She shook her head in disbelief.

Sarah picked her wedding dress and the two women walked home in the cold night.

"What should I wear?" Abby questioned.

"Well, I really don't have anything nice for you."

"I almost forgot, I picked out a lovely and simple dress at the shop. It would match perfectly with yours."

"Great then."

The young women walked the rest of the way thinking, not a word put in edgewise.

Jack walked along the river carrying Billy's clothing for the wedding. Sarah had made them herself.

When he reached Billy's front door, he knocked on it softly.

Billy answered and invited his old friend in. "Do you think they'll fit?" Billy questioned as Jack laid Billy's clothes on the kitchen table.

"Sure they will. Sarah made them my size and we're about the same." Jack was right. They fit perfectly. The outfit consisted of a white wool shirt along with gray cotton pants.

January first came and the wedding would be on that day. Abby was in Sarah's bedroom at her father's house.

"Here I come," Sarah warned from the hall. Sarah came around the corner smiling with big, bright eyes.

Abby couldn't help but gasp. Sarah looked like an angel sent down from Heaven. "Do you like it?" Sarah asked, grasping her gown and twirling around.

"You're so beautiful."

"Thank you."

Sarah wore a pearl necklace, which was her mother's. It was the family tradition. They shined like stars themselves. She had a full skirt on and she looked like a princess aside of an angel. Sarah sighed. "I'm nervous."

"Don't worry," Abby calmed her. "You're going to be great." Abby stood up from Sarah's bed to look at Sarah in the mirror as the bride did also.

Meanwhile, Billy knocked on Jack's door looking down the street to see if anyone was coming. It was a beautiful winter's day. The snow shone brightly with the sky bright blue.

Jack replied Billy's knock. "How do you feel?" was the first question Billy asked Jack.

Jack sighed. "Nervous, but excited," he explained as he buttoned up his shirt.

Katherine entered the room. "Hi," she greeted.

"Billy this is…"

"Katherine?" he was in shock.

"Yes?" She looked at Billy as if he had something wrong with him.

"Little Katherine?" He motioned a very small height. "Why, I remember you when you were…a baby!"

"You don't look anything like your portrait," she observed handing Billy his wanted poster.

"Hey…" he chimed. "I'm wanted. You told her?" he asked Jack, seriously.

"I had no choice," he explained, fixing his hair. "I told Sarah's father too. As well as the minister."

"Jack!"

"They would've recognized you anyway."

"You're right, but I still…"

"Don't worry."

"Okay. When are we leaving?" Billy asked.

"Now. I have a stagecoach coming." Jack turned to Katherine. "Are you ready?"

"Yes," Katherine replied.

"We're going to drop her off at Sarah's," Jack explained to Billy.

"Okay."

Katherine peeped outside. "The coach is here."

"All right," Jack said gathering his jacket. "Billy," he motioned to go before him. Billy did just that.

"Who is Jack's best man?" Abby asked Sarah.

"Billy," Sarah told her adjusting a bow on her dress.

"Billy?" Abby was surprised.

"Yes. Oh, Abby, I know about everything," Sarah said stopping what she was doing.

"You do?" Abby looked with wide-eyes.

"Yes."

"Sarah? Abby?" Katherine shouted from the kitchen.

"Up here!" Sarah shouted back.

Katherine came upstairs. "Hi. Wow, Sarah! Jack won't know what to say when he sees you. You look beautiful."

"Thank you," Sarah said.

"Abby, are you all right?" Katherine asked, knowing something was wrong.

"Do you know, too?" Abby questioned.

"About Billy? Yes, I do."

"Oh."

"It's all right. He was as mad as you are."

"You saw him?" she asked, anxious.

"Yes. A handsome fellow, isn't he?" Abby chuckled.

"Well," Sarah said looking at herself in the mirror one last time, "Should we go?"

"The stagecoach is here already. I told him that we'd be down soon," Katherine mentioned.

Sarah took a deep breath. "Ready?"

"Yes," Abby told her. "But are you?"

"More than ever," Sarah replied.

When they arrived at the church, Jack's stagecoach was already there.

Katherine, Abby, and Sarah went into the back room of the church to wait until they were to go up the aisle.

"Nervous?" Katherine asked Sarah.

"A bit," Sarah replied.

"You look lovely," Sarah sighed.

An usher popped his head in the doorway. "Almost ready, ladies? We're all set for you."

"Yes, I think we are," Sarah said looking around.

"Come on, then," he led.

The three girls followed the usher out into the back of the church where Billy and Jack waited, patiently.

Katherine sat down in the front next to Sarah's father. Next was Abby and Billy. Abby wrapped her arm around his and followed Katherine.

"You look beautiful," Jack said to Sarah.

She looked up at him with a promising smile. "Thank you." Sarah and Jack started toward the altar where they would be joined by marriage.

"I do," Jack answered the minister.

"And do you, Sarah Bridge, take Jack Canning to be your lawfully wedded husband, to have and to hold, through sickness and health, forever and ever, until death do you part?"

"I do," Sarah responded.

Abby couldn't help but look at Billy, who was sometimes meeting her gaze. When he looked, she would look away to help herself, for she was going to cry.

"You may kiss the bride," the minister announced with great joy. Jack kissed his new wife.

As Abby and Billy left the altar, Billy whispered, "I need to talk to you."

"No," she softly said back.

They reached the back of the church. Abby left and went outside because he wouldn't follow her out. There was too much of a risk involved. "Abby!" he shouted after her. He didn't care anymore and decided to follow her. "Abby," he yelled after her barging through the doors.

She looked back with anger, yet surprised he was following her.

"Please, Abby! Just listen! Hear what I have to say!" Billy ran to her, pulled her shoulder for her to turn around.

"I don't want to."

"Yes, you do. I know you."

"Maybe…but I guess I was wrong about you. I never knew you could murder somebody!" she screamed. She began to cry.

"I'm sorry," he apologized.

"Sorry doesn't help, Billy. It just doesn't."

They were standing in the street, staring like strangers at each other. "You better get inside. Before someone sees you," she whispered.

He took her hand in his. "Everything's going to be all right. I promise."

She took her hand back and looked at him. "Don't promise what you can't keep." Abby started walking toward the church, alone.

In a distance, Charles Cotter walked Main Street to meet an incoming ship from Boston. He saw Billy. He saw him standing in the street, blankly.

Not wanting to make a scene, he kept walking, thinking when was the best time to visit him.

Chapter 13

January 3, 1878

Sarah looked beautiful at the wedding. They were truly meant for each other. They are so in love.

I was hoping for that with Billy. I just don't know if I could face him again. How foolish I acted after the wedding! Yes, that's right. He's back in town.

Hattie is alive! They found her down by the river. I am so happy they found her. Well, I must go now.

Abby

Abby and Katherine sat in front of the fire one snowy night. "Where's Sarah tonight?" Abby asked.

"She went to visit her father for a while," Katherine answered.

"Oh, Jack went with her?" Katherine nodded. "I have to go home, but I won't leave you alone."

"It's all right, Abby, I'll be fine."

"Don't be silly, I'll wait. Besides, they're probably on their way now."

Just then, Jack walked through the door with the widest grin Abby has ever seen on his face. "Why are you so happy?" Abby wondered, curiously.

"Sarah...and me...we're going to have a baby!" he exclaimed.

Sarah, then, walked in as he made the announcement. "Oh, Jack! I wanted to see their faces. You told me you'd wait until I was present."

"I'm sorry," he apologized. "I'm just so happy."

Sarah laughed, taking him in her arms. "You're going to be a great father," she whispered.

"You think?" She nodded, in open admiration of the man she married.

"Congratulations, to both of you," Abby said.

"I'm going to be an aunt?" Katherine anticipated.

Jack nodded.

"I hate to leave, but I really should get going," Abby told.

"Would you like me to walk you to home?" Jack asked, kindly.

"No, you can celebrate. Thank you, though."

It was snowing lightly as Abby walked home. It was late and she knew her "parents" would be asleep. Approaching the general store, Abby saw the downstairs window illuminated by candlelight. She knew it was odd for them to be up. Why wouldn't they be asleep?

Billy.

Maybe they found out he was home. What if she was too late? What if they just got back? Abby ran to the building.

As she entered the kitchen, looking drastically around, Abby saw her "mother" dressed warmly. "Where are you going?" Abby questioned.

"None of your business!" she snapped.

Charles entered wide-eyed. "Go to bed!" he raised his voice to Abby. Abby nodded, yes. She went to the stairs and climbed them. At the top, she sat listening to their conversation.

"Do you have the gun?" Cecile Cotter asked.

"Yes, it's out back. Let's go finish him off," her "father" snarled.

In an instant, the lantern left the room, making the kitchen pitch black. Abby stumbled downstairs planning as she rushed to one back room of the store.

She found the case where Charles' guns were kept. She took hold of a rifle and went out the front door.

Peeking around the corner to see if there was any human activity, Abby waited patiently to go warn Billy. When the woods were clear of light, Abby tiptoed in and followed the path cautiously with the rifle in her hand.

Abby arrived the banks of the river looking down the small river for the murderers.

No one was there.

Abby waded in, soaking herself in ice-cold water and made her way to the opposite bank. She held her gun over her head to keep it dry.

She had to hurry. Time was precious. Abby ran carelessly through the woods seeking Old Mann Rock. When Abby reached the rock, her "parents'" boat was tied to a tree and no light shown in the woods.

Was she too late?

She grasped the rifle tighter and ran along the road to Billy's house. As she approached his home, she observed the door wide-opened. She heard shouting and she was afraid. Abby put her fears away and continued inside Billy's house. In the parlor, Billy sat with fear and relief, to see it was Abby.

Charles Cotter held a gun pointing to Billy. "Abigail?" Cecile turned around with shock in her face. Her "father" turned also.

Abby stuck the rifle up at them with her hands shaking for she had no idea, what-so-ever how to work that thing. "Leave," she demanded, straight out.

"You get out of here," Charles fiercely roared after her.

"No," she said. "You get out of here."

Abby stared in her "father's" eyes, deceiving him in every way. Charles and Cecile's back were turned to Billy. He motioned to Abby. Abby saw him in the corner of her eye.

He was going to do something.

Billy stood up quietly and jumped on the murderer. Charles was knocked to the ground as Cecile tried to pick him up. The rifle slid on the floor to Abby. She picked it up and threw it to Billy.

Billy pointed it to the Cotters. "All right," Charles agreed, "we'll leave. But don't worry, we'll be back." The couple walked to the door and out into the snowy night. Billy and Abby followed them to make sure they left.

They did.

As soon as they were gone, Abby dropped the gun and held Billy with all her might.

"I'm sorry," she apologized.

"Don't be," he whispered, back. Abby closed her eyes, for this is where she wanted to be for the rest of her life.

Chapter 14

January 5, 1878

I am so happy now. Could life be more perfect? Billy's finally home. I can't wipe the never-ending smile off of my face. It is impossible.

I don't think I'll ever be able to leave here. Once again, it is Heaven.

My "parents" haven't been back yet and I pray they won't ever return.

All my worries are behind me as I lay next to Billy on the rock. I know soon, though, reality is destined to come back.

Abby

Billy and Abby were just lying on the cold rock, as the snow gloriously rained down on them. Abby sat up. She rolled to her stomach and looked at Billy.

"Life will never be the same. You know that, right?" Abby asked.

Billy nodded, afraid of saying anything he might regret. "I know."

"So how can you pretend like it will always be like this?"

"I don't know," he replied, looking away from her. She laid down again on her back.

Billy reached for her hand and held it tightly. "I can pretend...I can pretend because I know you'll never leave."

She turned her head to look at him and smiled. "That's the answer I was hoping to hear."

As they rocked together on their rockers, later that night, Abby read from the Bible. The fire roared before them illuminating their faces with a warm glow.

Billy thought about Abby's life when he was in Enfield. *Why hadn't she told him about the rape? Did she not want to frighten him?*

He was perplexed.

Billy watched her and time seemed to slow down. He watched her every move and how every few seconds she'd pause and look at him. She'd smile and then continue reading.

He hadn't realized how much he had missed her until tonight. He couldn't live without her. He needed her for the rest of his life.

Abby closed the book. "I'm going to stop. I'm tired," she said.

"All right," he said, shyly. He hadn't known why.

Abby went to the sofa and laid down. She closed her eyes. "Good night," Billy said pouring water on the fire.

"Good night," she said in return as he kissed her on the forehead. He proceeded upstairs.

The next day, Abby decided to go back home for a while. "I'll be back," she said.

"Okay," he replied, helping her put on her cloak.

"Thank you," she smiled. They were at the bank of the river where he always dropped her off.

Abby walked the woods looking around as she always had. Lately, she had run, not paying much attention to the forest that surrounded her. As she approached her house, Abby felt nervous and hoped her "parents" wouldn't be home, for they would never let her leave again.

She mainly went back to see if she had a letter from Nick. There it was, lying on the kitchen table waiting for her to open a bad future. A future that was unwanted. She wanted to burn it. She despised all his letters and wanted to write for him not go come.

She carefully opened the envelope. The letter inside read:

January 4, 1878

Abby,

    How are you doing? I am leaving today to go to New York City. So you don't have to bother writing back to me because next time I go home, you will be with me.
    I am spending two days in the city because my cousin, Violet, is marrying. But then I will leave for you. I should arrive the 7th or the 8th.
    I really don't know when we will leave for Harvard, but we will need to leave before the 12th because the 13th is when our wedding will occur.
    I am so excited to see your beauty again.

    I Love You,
    Nick

She wept softly reading the letter. *No, no, no!* She wanted to scream. *It wasn't supposed to work out like this.* She couldn't reach him. She couldn't tell him she didn't want to marry him.

She had to talk to someone. There was no one. She'd only hurt Billy, Katherine was too young to understand, Sarah didn't know really what was going on, and Jack, well Jack, would tell her to leave him at the altar.

There was no one. No one at all. She didn't know exactly what to do. She decided to tell him when he arrived. He'd be there in about two days. She'd tell him then.

She didn't know what exactly to do.

When she got her grip, she wiped her eyes, took a deep breath, and went to her bedroom. She took a clean dress from her closet, not knowing when she'd be back. But she knew she would. Her "parents" would come and get her.

Abby went downstairs listening closely to hear if someone was home. She didn't hear anything. The coast was clear. She crept outside into the beautiful day, taking it all in along with the crisp air of January. She loved blue-skied days. They were too pleasant to be with.

Abby went to the river. She had to cross the freezing water. She held her belongings over her head so she wouldn't get them wet.

Walking along the banks of the fast-flowing river, Abby didn't know what to say to Billy about Nick. She didn't want to hurt him. But she didn't know how to prevent that from happening.

He was on the rock waiting for her. Billy saw her coming and smiled. "I'm sorry I didn't come back."

"It's all right," she reassured.

Abby set Nick's letter on the rock on top of her dress as she climbed up. "Who's the letter from?" Billy asked, sounding as if he knew who it was from.

"Um…" she sighed, knowing she couldn't keep the truth from him any longer. "Nick." Her head fell.

"Oh." He looked away, hurt.

"He's coming, either tomorrow or the day after."

She looked at him to see his reaction, but only saw the back of his head. Abby put her hand on his. "Then we're going to leave for Boston where we'll be married."

"So soon?" he whispered.

"You knew I was leaving. Why are you mad now?"

"I was angry before."

"But, Billy…you are acting as if I've never said anything to you about this."

"It's because I had forgotten. I figured if I forgot, then it wouldn't come true."

Abby sighed.

"I just don't like how you keep secrets away from me."

"Billy, I have told you everything," she argued.

"Everything?"

"Yes."

"You're lying!" he shouted.

"How so?"

"You never told me about the morning you woke up in the alleyway, scared, naked, not knowing where you were."

She looked as if she was about to cry. She replied, calmly, "I wanted to forget that."

"Abby…you don't know how hurt I was when Jack told me. I thought you didn't trust me."

She turned away. "It's not that."

"Then what is it?" he asked, kindly.

"It's embarrassing."

"Oh, Abby, you don't have to worry. We can work this out. You don't need to keep anything from me."

She started bursting with tears as she turned back to him. "I never had the chance to cry."

"I understand."

"I feel so dirty."

"Do you know who did it?"

She shook her head. "No idea."

"Well, I'm not going to accuse anyone, but…"

"I know you think it's Nick."

"Maybe, Abby."

"Or maybe it was a foolish drunk stumbling around that night. I don't want to think of Nick doing that."

"Okay. I understand."

"Thank you."

"For what?"

"For being so good about this," she said.

"No problem."

"I think we should go inside. It's getting dark."

Abby stood up, picked her belongings off of the rock and followed Billy to his house. Inside, Billy made a fire, while Abby took jarred beats from the basement. That would be their dinner.

After dinner, they sat in their rocking chairs. Abby decided to read Billy his father's journal. He enjoyed it very much. When Abby was tired of reading, she closed his journal. "We'll save some for tomorrow night."

"You can sleep in my bed tonight and I'll sleep down here."

"Oh, no, Billy. You were away and I'm sure you miss your bed."

"It's fine. Don't worry," he assured.

"Are you sure?" she asked.

"Yes."

Abby stood up from her rocking chair and went to Billy. They kissed each other Good night. "Good night," she said.

"Good night," he replied, watching her climb the stairs.

The morning was bright. Sunrays poured in from the skies above. Abby and Billy moved their rocking chairs on the front porch. They rocked for hours, talking about endless things. Once in a while, Billy would get something for Rosie to eat.

"So," Billy started. "What are we going to do?"

"About what?" she asked.

"Nick," he replied, firmly.

"Oh." She looked down. "I guess I go with him. I don't know."

"But…"

"Billy, you have to understand. It's the only way. We both messed up."

"There has to be another way."

She put her hand on his and shook her head. "There isn't."

"Don't you believe…Abby, don't you believe in true love?" he asked her, looking in her eyes.

She turned away. "Yes."

"So, why…"

"Billy, everyday, people are going through this."

"But why do we?"

"It just works out that way."

"It doesn't have to. I know it doesn't."

"Can't you accept it? It's not all my fault. It's yours too. They're going to come and look for you. They're going to put you in jail. We both need to move on."

"I wish it wasn't this way," he said.

"Me neither," she tried to smile.

"I have missed these days," Abby said as she and Billy sat on the rock watching the sun go down.

"Me too," he agreed. Billy couldn't help look at her because of the way she was. The way the sun streaked her hair with magnificent gold strands. That's what he had missed the most. "How about…"

"Billy…" Abby had cut off. She looked pale and frightened. "A boat," she pointed.

"Come on," he rose quickly, helping her up at the same time. "Let's go."

"Where?" she panicked.

"I don't know. Just come on," he ran into the woods. They hid in the forest as the murderers accompanied by guests climbed the rock.

"All right, Abby and Billy. I know you're here. I saw you from a distance," Charles said.

Billy looked at Abby. She was breathing hard, but softly. "I have the sheriff here."

Abby's head fell. "No," she whispered.

"It's okay," Billy said.

The sheriff and another man looked around, as well as Charles. "Come out, you two. Your secret is out."

"I'm doing this because of you," Billy whispered in Abby's ear. "Stay low." Billy jumped out of the woods.

"I give up. You have me." Abby was in shock. What was he doing?

"Good, boy, you came out. Now, let's get going." The sheriff took Billy in the boat and the four men rowed away.

Abby immediately jumped out of the woods, crying. Was that a terrible joke? Why would he do that? "No," she whimpered. "Not again."

She quickly ran to her canoe and drifted away, then poling the river. She needed to go to Jack. He'd know what to do.

As Abby approached the fork of the river, she saw them in their small boat going to the main port.

She went the way she always had, in case they spotted her. Abby leaped out of the beat-up canoe, not bothering to tie it. She didn't care anymore.

She ran and ran, gasping for oxygen on the way. She got to Jack's house and pounded with her fists, on the front door. Sarah answered. "Hello, Abby. Are you all right?"

"Sarah? Where's Jack?" she panted.

"Out back. Why?" Sarah asked, curiously.

"I don't have time to talk," Abby apologized, running to their backyard.

Jack was splitting wood. He saw Abby run hysterically to him. "Abby?"

"Jack...it's Billy..."

"What, Abby?" She breathed heavily.

"Slow down..."

"They took him away," she cried.

"Who?"

"The sheriff...my parents...a man..." She fell to her knees. "He gave himself to them. I made a mistake. I'm sorry."

"Whoa," he calmed, kneeling down next to her. "It's okay."

She shook her head, swallowing. "No...it's not. It'll never be."

"Yes, Abby, it will. I promise," he assured.

She wiped her tears away. "So what do we do?"

They had no plan. They didn't know what was going to happen. They weren't sure of anything.

Jack and Abby headed to the town prison by the shore that night. Not knowing where Billy was exactly, they snuck around the jailhouse, peeking in each barred-up window to see if Billy was visible.

He wasn't visible in any cell. "We need to go in," Abby realized.

"Abby!" Jack whispered, stopping her. "What are you going to say to them?"

She shook her head. "I don't know. But I have to talk to him."

"They'll never let you in," he told her.

"Then how do you think I should get in there?"

"Tell them…tell them…you are here to discuss his property claim," he suggested, pulling her hood over her head. "Put this on."

"Okay." She took a deep breath and turned to leave. "What if they recognize me?" She turned back quickly.

"They won't."

"How are you so sure?"

"Abby, trust me. They won't."

"Okay." Abby continued inside.

"Excuse me," Abby said, trying to get the sleeping guard's attention. She wasn't about to go in without consulting him. What if he woke up while she was talking to Billy? "Excuse me!" she shouted.

"What? Where?" the guard jumped, waking up immediately.

"Hello," Abby smiled.

"Yes, pretty girl?" the guard grinned.

"Hi…um, I'm here to talk to Billy Sanson. He was taken in this evening."

"Oh, yes, he was."

"What business do you have?"

"I need to talk about his property claim."

"At this time of night?" the guard inquired.

"I was sent here to talk to him as quickly as I could."

"I think you're foolin' me, but, since you're so pretty, I guess I'll let you in," he told her.

"Thank you so much," Abby appreciated. The sleazy guard unlocked the door that led to the cells and guided her inside. Billy was lying down in his bed, awake.

"You have a visitor," the man mentioned to Billy as he sat up from the bed. The man unlocked the barred-up door. "Some property claims woman."

Abby's eyes grew large to tell Billy to play along. "Thank you," she said, letting herself in.

The guard stood outside the cell. "Um…" Abby started. "Aren't you going to leave?"

"No. It's my job to watch the cell at all times, pretty girl."

Abby sighed and went up to him. "But what if someone goes into your office, takes the keys to someone's cell, unlocks it for them, and let them go? Would you want that to happen? Don't you trust me? I won't do anything," she said innocently.

The guard smirked. "I guess you're right, pretty girl."

"All right, then. Thank you." He turned and left.

When he was out of sight, Abby immediately hugged Billy. "Why?" she whispered.

"What do you mean?" he questioned, letting her go.

"Why did you give yourself to him?"

"Because of you. I want you to be happy."

"But you being away from me, it isn't happiness, Billy."

"But you said…" he argued.

"Never mind what I said." Abby sat down on Billy's bed. He followed.

"I go on trial tomorrow."

"For what?"

"Murder. They want me to…to be hung."

She looked down with anger, shaking her head. "No. They can't."

"They can."

"How are you so calm about all of this?" she sobbed.

"So that will be good. Do that with my land," he said.

She looked at him strangely. Billy motioned with his eyes this time that the guard was present. "Okay, pretty girl, time is up," the guard told her.

Abby stood up, sniffling and exited the cell. The guard examined her face. "Oh," she sobbed. "Those land claims. They're so sad."

The man looked at Billy with a weird curiosity on his face. Billy shrugged his shoulders.

"Jack?" Abby called, looking around when she was outside.

"Abby," Jack replied from a shrub. Abby went to him. "I'm stuck."

Abby chuckled a little bit. She took his arm and pulled him out. "What do you know?" he asked, impatiently.

"He's going on trial tomorrow."

"Tomorrow?"

"Yes," she replied. "They want to put him to death."

Jack sighed. "Oh no."

"Exactly. What do we do now?" She looked for answers on his face.

"I don't know. The only thing we really can do is wait."

"Wait for what?"

"We wait to see what happens, Abby. I'm sorry, we can't do anything else."

"Yeah, well, I want everything to be okay again."

"I already have promised that," he reminded.

"Yes, I know. But I don't see it coming true."

"It will," he said. "I know it will."

The next day, Jack woke Abby up from a horrible night's sleep. She had only slept two hours. She dreaded this day. The day Billy would be sentenced for a murder he had committed. The sentencing was being held in a court in Massachusetts, seeing that was the closest courtroom the officials could find.

Abby was sure her "parents" would be present. No doubt was on her mind. Abby and Jack decided to take Rosie there. Walking would be too time consuming. It wasn't light out yet and Jack wanted to slip away before Sarah woke up. She would tell him not to go. He left her a note stating Abby went home and he had to work early. She would believe it.

Just as dawn approached, the two were off, dreading what they knew would be bad news when they arrived.

Court had already started. Jack and Abby quietly snuck in, sitting in the back. Billy did not have a good lawyer because he knew that Billy committed the crime. Billy was called up to the stand.

"Did you or did you not murder Tom Marshall?" the arrogant lawyer asked him.

"I did," Billy said, looking away. The audience gasped and talked amongst themselves.

"Why?" the man inquired.

"Because," Billy answered.

"Because why?"

"Because he murdered my parents."

The lawyer laughed. The audience laughed. The judge even laughed. "Order! Order! Order!" the judge shouted, finally realizing what position he was in.

"You're not supposed to lie," the man questioning him said.

"I'm not, sir," Billy shrugged.

"No further questions."

"All right then," the judge started. "Recess for five minutes while the sentence is made." The people in the pews got up and started talking and walking around.

"Are you okay?" Jack asked Abby.

She was in a daze. "No."

Jack wrapped his arms around her. "My promise is still standing."

"They all think he's a fool. They all think he's lying. But he's not. He's not lying."

"I know," he whispered.

Five minutes later, the judge came back to his stand. "The jury has decided to put Billy Sanson, the murderer of Tom Marshall, to death. He will be hung on January 13, 1878, in front of his hometown."

Abby couldn't believe it. "No!" she shouted. "Please! No!" Everyone looked at her, shocked. Especially Billy.

"Don't do this to me. Please don't!" she cried. "He doesn't deserve it."

"Abby!" Jack said, trying to keep her stable. "It's okay," he whispered in her ear as he hugged her tightly.

"No, Jack," she softly cried. "I don't believe you anymore."

Chapter 15

January 7, 1878

Crying! It's all I can do. It's all I can bear. My world has been turned upside down. I fear I will not be strong enough to turn it over.

I wish this never happened. I wish my heart didn't ache so. I wish this could all be over.

Abby

Jack held her until her whimpering stopped. They were seated outside the courthouse, wishing what they just had heard was all a lie.

She closed her eyes as she recited small prayers in her head. Nothing could make her feel better.

Nothing.

Except for maybe Billy. He was the thought that made her get through this. A part of her realized she was only living on that thought and she didn't have hope. She didn't have hope they'd come out of this alive; both of them.

"Jack?" Abby whispered, pulling away from him, her eyes swollen.

"Yeah?"

"It's time to go." She looked out into the horizon and noticed the sun was setting as well as every color that it possessed.

"I think it is." He lifted to his feet and then helped Abby up. They walked to Rosie who seemed quite happy to see them. As they ventured back to their hometown, Abby continued to feel restless; dead.

They arrived at Jack's house in the darkness of the night. "Would you like to stay here tonight?" Jack offered.

Abby shook her head, then sighed. "No thanks. I'm going to take old Rosie back home." She patted the horse.

"All right. Good night then, Abby," Jack said, entering his home. "Bye."

Abby lifted herself onto Rosie. She kicked the horse's side gently to tell her to go.

Abby walked Main Street the next morning. She thought it would be nice to stroll the bustling small town before leaving with Nick for Boston. The day was beautiful. Blue sky flooded the earth, suffocating it in its overbearing beauty. It was windy, which made it much cooler that it truly was.

Clutching tightly to her cloak, Abby made her way through the town. She was going to Parson Gowns to pick up her dresses. Abby opened the door to the dressmaker's shop and saw him.

It was Nick.

He turned to see who was entering and saw Abby, standing there, staring wide-eyed at him. He could hardly believe it himself. "Abby!" He rushed toward her and slipped his arms around her.

"Nick," she tried saying with enthusiasm.

"I was going to come by your house right after I paid Miss Parson her money."

"Really?" She didn't know what to do or what to say.

"Yeah." He was so happy to see her.

"I was just coming by to pick them up."

He took a deep breath. "You're so beautiful. More than I remembered."

She wanted to cry. Why had she led him on to think she loved him? "Thank you." She walked passed him to see Amelia Parson, so she could fetch her dresses.

Miss Parson gave her the dresses along with her wedding gown and Nick paid for them.

"You don't seem happy to see me," Nick said as they left the building.

She shook her head and smiled. "No, I am, Nick. It's just that I'm surprised to see you. That's all."

"Well, you knew I was coming today. Didn't you receive my letter?"

She nodded. "Yes."

"Then why are you so surprised?"

She decided to make the best of it. "You just caught me off guard. That's all," she smiled.

"Oh," he said, bewildered. He leaned in to kiss her. Abby moved out of the way. "What's wrong?" he questioned. She looked up at him, not wanting to hurt him in any way. "I'm not in the mood," she continued walking.

"Oh."

"Yeah."

"Did you know Christina had her baby yesterday?" he asked, trying to make conversation as he walked beside her.

"Really? No, I didn't hear that."

"It's a girl. Her name is Laura," he told her.

"Is she cute?"

"Adorable."

"That's great, Uncle Nick."

His eyes widened. "Oh, I know. Can you believe it? I am an uncle. One day, I hope to be called Daddy." He smiled at Abby.

She didn't know what to say. "Yeah," was all she could think of.

They decided on Abby going to his house, and then they said goodbye for a while. Abby said she needed to change. It was an excuse to be alone.

Abby snuck inside the house, cautious that someone might be home. Her "father" was. She looked at him with anger and hatred and then left. She showed no fear. She was proud of herself that she was able to do this.

Abby went into her bedroom. Constance was asleep in her cot, her dress drenched with blood. She quickly walked to her younger sister and started to wake her up. "Abby!" her father bellowed from downstairs. "Get down here!"

Abby sat up from the side of Constance's bed. She backed away slowly, staring at her sister, knowing why he was calling her down. She closed her eyes as she shuffled down the stairs.

There her "father" was, whip in hand, standing before her with rage and fury in his eyes. He whipped her hard. She flinched as the leather smacked down on her back, cutting into her flesh. She cried out for the pain was too much she could possibly bear. *I'll get you for this*, she thought as his anger slapped her bare back.

"You stay away from that boy Billy. He's a murderer! Besides, you're getting married and going to Boston. Finally, we're getting rid of you! You've been nothing but trouble. We should've never taken you. Your parents probably faked their death and ran away, not wanting you anymore!"

Abby burst out in tears, wanting so badly to trade positions with him. She knew well enough not to talk back to him.

When he finished, Abby was soaked. Soaked in her blood as well as tears. She crawled up the stairs, wanting to get away from him.

Constance was awake and undressing herself as Abby opened to door to come in. Constance was startled.

"Sorry. I didn't mean to scare you," she said, hurting badly. Abby fell to her knees.

Constance ran to her sister. "Oh, Abby, are you all right?"

"I'll be fine," she said as Constance helped her up.

The door slammed shut downstairs. Constance went to the window. She saw Charles leave the house. "Good, he's gone. I'll be right back." Constance flew out of the door.

A few minutes later, she returned, pulling the washbasin in. "A nice bath is in need," Constance said.

Abby smiled with relief. "You're right."

"Hattie and them get one everyday and now I only get one every month as you do." Abby carefully peeled her dress off her sore body. "I have water downstairs heating up," Constance added.

"Great."

"You can wash first," Constance offered.

"Oh, no…you go ahead. It was your idea."

Constance grinned. "Thank you."

After Constance bathed, it was Abby's turn. *It felt so good*, she thought.

"Abby, are you leaving?" Constance asked as Abby cleaned her body with a cloth. "Are you going to Boston?"

"Yeah, I guess I am," Abby said, feeling guilty.

"Why?" she asked, tears welling up in her eyes.

"I'm getting married."

"Oh," Constance blankly said, continuing to comb her hair. "But…"

"What?" her younger sister's eyes widened at the sound of her sister's rebuttal.

"But I don't know if I'm going to."

"Oh." Constance laid the hairbrush on the dresser and sat on her cot. "I'm going to run away, then."

Abby frowned, not believing what she was hearing. "What? Why?"

"I don't think I can survive him beating me over and over. I only stayed because of you. Hattie's different now because Mommy and Daddy only pay attention to her. No one loves me anymore."

Abby stepped out of the tub, drying herself with a towel. "Constance, you can't."

"I have to. I can't live like this."

"Where are you going to go?" Abby inquired, hoping to stump her younger sister and to make her think twice about leaving.

"Down the Connecticut. I'll follow it and make myself a better life."

Abby shook her head. "No…no…Absolutely not. A thirteen-year-old girl out there all alone, is not much appreciated." Abby thought Constance and Billy were so much alike. They had the same dreams.

"I can make it," Constance argued.

"Listen," Abby started sitting down next to Constance on the cot. "If I don't get married, I might be headed somewhere else. If I don't go to Boston, I'll bring you along. All right?"

Constance nodded. "Promise?"

"I promise," Abby replied. "You won't say anything to anyone."

"Okay," she nodded yet again. "What if you do get married?"

"If I do get married...If I do..." Abby sighed. "...I'm not quite sure. But I'll think of something."

"Okay."

"Now, I have to go get ready."

"For what?"

"I have to go meet up with Nick, my husband-to-be."

Abby sorted through her new dresses. She wanted to look presentable. She picked a lavender-colored one out. The lace collared the dress as well as the end of the sleeves. She slipped on black boots over her feet. She felt new as well as beautiful. She combed out her long hair, gathering all the strands into a bun.

"You look lovely," Constance commented.

"Really?" Abby asked, hoping it was true.

"Uh-huh." Abby sighed in relief and said goodbye to her sister. Then she grabbed her cloak on the way out.

Abby knocked on the door of Nick's house. Christina, with her baby in her arms, answered the door. She looked exhausted. "Hi, Christina," Abby greeted. "Congratulations. She's beautiful."

"Thank you, Abby," she sighed. "Come in. Nick is this way."

Christina was being so nice. Maybe it was because she was so tired or maybe there was no reason at all. The new mother shut the door behind Abby. Nick saw Abby immediately and stood up. "Hi."

"Hi," she replied, taking her cloak off.

"Is that a new dress?" Nick questioned. "One from Parson Gowns?" Abby nodded. "It looks beautiful on you."

Abby smiled. "Thank you."

"I'm so upset," Christina sat down next to Nick, "I won't see you two get married."

"I wish you could be there," Nick said.

"Me too," Abby lied.

Abby was sore. She saw how much anger her father held when he whipped her today. What for? Because she knew his secret? "All my friends can't wait to meet you, Abby. They're very excited a beautiful lady is coming to campus. As am I."

"I can't wait," she tried to sound cheerful, hoping he couldn't see right through her.

"When are you planning on marrying Henry, Christina?" Abby inquired.

She was in a daze; not knowing Abby was talking to her. "Christina?" Nick said, trying to get her attention.

"Yes?" she replied, looking the same way. There was something obviously wrong with her.

"Abby asked you a question. Be kind to our guest. You're being very rude!" he snapped.

"I'm sorry!" she shouted back, raising herself from the sofa. "I'm sorry," she calmed, as soon as she looked into Nick's eyes and sat down.

"Continue, Abby…" she said, looking back to her.

Abby didn't know if she should say anything, but decided to. "When are you and Henry planning on marrying?" she repeated.

"Hopefully never," Christina frowned.

"Oh," was all Abby could say.

"Well, excuse me," Nick said, standing up. "I need to meet Mr. Wardell at the bank. Bye, Abby," Nick called after her, exiting out the door.

"Abby?" Christina turned to her quickly as soon as Nick shut the door behind him. "I need your help."

"What is it?" Abby asked, not knowing if she should have.

"I'm leaving."

"Leaving?" Abby didn't know what she was getting at.

"Yeah. I'm running away. I can't take this anymore." She sounded as if she was insane. "Laura will have a much better life without me."

Abby shook her head. "No…no, Christina, you're wrong. A girl needs her mother."

"What do you know?" Christina asked freshly. "You have one!"

She wasn't too good of a mother, Abby thought. *She isn't even my mother*. "Well I can't take it anymore. I fear I'm going to do something to hurt her."

"You can't take what?" Abby didn't understand.

"I can't take Nick. He's different now. I can't take my father. He's on the verge of dying. I can't take Henry. I can't take Henry's damn parents. I need to get away."

"What do you want me to do?"

"Take her. Henry doesn't know. He'll just think I left with her."

"Take her? Christina, I'm barely sixteen yet. I have enough problems in my life already. I can't."

"Do something with her. I can't take care of her." Christina put Laura in Abby's arms. She stood up and left out the door. Before she went, she said: "Thank you, Abby. Tell Nick nothing. Goodbye." And she slammed the door shut behind her.

Was that a dream? Did Christina Porter really abandon her beautiful baby girl because she couldn't take it anymore? God, what was wrong with these people?

Abby didn't know what to do. Laura started crying. Her lungs were small, but the noise seemed to fill the sky. "Shh…" Abby rocked her, trying to get the small baby back to sleep. When Laura slept peacefully, Abby went into Nick's bedroom, in search of a blanket to wrap the new human in. She would take her to Henry.

Abby held Laura close to her body, trying to keep her warm. The wind howled in her ear, chilling Abby's spine. The day was a bit after sunset when Abby reached the farm. Abby knocked at the front door.

Henry answered. "Abby?" he said, surprised to see her.

"Hi, Henry." She stood there, waiting for him to ask her in. He did this as soon as he realized her hesitation.

When they were warmly inside, Henry offered her a seat. "You and Nick had a baby? Last time I saw you, you didn't seem pregnant," Henry smiled, making a joke.

Abby smiled looking down at the sleeping child. "No, we didn't. Um...she's yours."

Henry's eyes widened. "What?"

"She's yours, Henry."

"Christina wasn't due for two weeks."

"She's an early bird," Abby commented, looking at his child.

"Her? What's her name?"

"Laura."

Henry rushed to his child. Abby gently handed her over to him. "She's beautiful," he smiled, not believing it. He fell in love with her at first sight.

"She is."

Henry suddenly frowned. "So, why are you bringing her to me? Where's Christina? Did she..."

Abby cut him off, not wanting him to think of that. "No, she's fine." He took a deep breath and looked back down at his daughter.

"She...she...ran away."

"What?"

"She said she couldn't take it anymore and she needed to leave."

"We were supposed to..."

"I know. I don't know how she could do that. Laura's beautiful."

"Thank you."

"She just handed her to me. I didn't know what to do with her, so I brought her here. I hope that's all right?"

"You did the right thing. Thank you," he praised. "Mama! Come in here," he shouted out to her.

Henry's mother entered the room. "Is it?" the pudgy woman asked, stopping in her tracks when she saw Henry holding Laura.

"Yes, Mama. She's Laura," Henry told her. The woman darted toward her granddaughter.

As they adored Laura, Abby slipped out the front door, not drawing any attention to herself. The moon was big when Abby saw it. A full moon, in fact.

Abby started toward Billy's home. She was tired from the big day. Abby couldn't help but think what kind of person would leave their newborn baby like that. She suddenly realized, people like Christina would.

Abby decided to go see if Billy's cell had a window this time. Chances were that he had been moved because he was going to be put to death.

Abby walked around the prison peering into each window to see if Billy was in any of them. About halfway around the building, Abby spotted Billy and ran to the window. "Billy!" she whispered and shouted at the same time. He was asleep. "No...no...no!" She looked all around for something to throw inside to wake him up.

Abby found some stones and threw one to the floor. Billy fidgeted. She threw another. He was finally awakened and his attention was drawn to Abby. "Abby!" he said, going to the window. Abby put her arms through the bars. He took her hands in his. "I was so afraid I wouldn't see you again!"

"Don't worry! That wouldn't be possible."

"That's good to know."

"Yeah, I guess it is," she smiled. "I have to get you out of here."

"Now that's impossible."

"No it's not. I thought about it. I've figured how to get you out of here."

"How?" Abby told him her plan. She had thought it up on her way from Henry's.

The next day, Abby woke up tired. Tired from the day before. Tired from knowing what she was going to do that day.

She had an unsure plan. She didn't know if it would work. She could only pray. Abby got up from her cot. It was late in the morning, she realized. The sun was standing halfway in the sky. She pulled her nightgown over her head, wondering what she was going to wear. She only knew it had to be revealing. Abby picked a party dress from her new wardrobe. It was cut low, revealing the amount she wanted to. She fixed her hair in a bun, but seductively let strands hang loosely around her face. Abby took her cloak and left the house to seek Billy.

Abby went to his window. She wouldn't be able to help him escape until late tonight, so the guard would be sleepy. She decided to wait all day with Billy and talk to him.

"Hi," she whispered, crouching down behind a shrub.

"Abby." Billy went to the window. "I thought you weren't going to come."

"I woke up late."

Billy placed a chair underneath the window, where he'd sit, looking like he wasn't doing anything, but at the same time, enjoying Abby's company. "Oh."

"I have news."

"You do?" he smirked, loving to hear her voice.

"It's not big news. Remember Christina?" Billy frowned. "The pregnant girl. Very seductive. She kissed you?"

"Oh, yeah. When you said she kissed me, I remembered immediately," Billy teased.

"That's not funny." A guard walked by the cell and Abby quickly moved her head, hoping he didn't see her nor hear her.

"Well," Abby started when the coast was clear, "she had her baby two days ago. The father of her baby is a nice man named Henry, and they were supposed to marry each other. And yesterday... I know you're not going to like it, but I visited Nick for a while. He had a meeting with the bank or something and he needed to go. So he left and Christina was there. She was very miserable. She told me she couldn't take it anymore and she needed to leave. She gave me her new baby, Laura, and just left."

"Who would do that to their baby like that?"

"She would. So I brought it to Henry. I know she'll find love with him."

"That's good," he smiled.

"Yeah," she agreed. There was a long pause. Abby broke the silence. "I'm sorry," she whispered.

"For what?" he asked, wanting to hold her hand, but couldn't.

"This," she began to whimper.

"It's not your fault, Abby. Never ever think that."

"I don't know if this plan will work. I really don't."

"It will," was all he said. "Trust me."

"I trust you."

Abby stayed there for the day. They talked about everything. Liz. Enfield. How it was like to live somewhere else in this big world.

"My father beat me yesterday."

"Again?"

"Yes."

"I'm sorry, Abby," he apologized for the man he despised. For his wrongdoing.

"He knows I know. I just know one day he'll be punished for what he's done. I'm going to do it and I will enjoy every second of it."

"I know you will."

"He told me how much he'd be glad I'm leaving because I was so much trouble and he thinks my real parents faked their death and left because they didn't want me anymore."

"It's not true, Abby. Don't let him get to you like that," Billy assured.

Abby wiped her tears. "Your words are always what I want to hear. That's all I really needed to hear. Thank you."

Meanwhile, at the Cotter household, Constance made her way down the stairs for supper. As usual, no words were spoken and the same chores were done after they finished.

When Hattie and their mother left the kitchen, Constance began to follow. "Constance," Charles said, stopping her before she left. Constance turned toward her father. "Why did you take the washbasin up to your room? You already had your bath for this month."

"I'm sorry. It won't happen again." She turned to leave.

"You're right, it won't." Constance heard the slapping of the whip on the table. "Come here."

Should I make the run for it? Where will I go? He'd eventually catch up to me and maybe do worse to me. This was all she thought.

It was worth a try.

Constance darted out the front door and into the cold night, an angry Charles after her. She tripped, but bobbed back up on her feet racing the wind. He finally gave up after a few hundred yards. She took a deep breath with relief. Where would she go now? She didn't know where Abby was. Then it finally came up on her. She'd go to the town orphanage. Constance made her way to the orphanage, when she started to stride by the Canning's house.

Maybe Abby was there. She had mentioned Jack and Katherine Canning before. Constance knocked on the door. Sarah answered with a smile. "Hi," Constance began, looking in the house. "Is Abby here?"

Sarah shook her head. "No, she's not. I'm sorry."

Constance frowned. "Okay, thank you. If she does come by, will you tell her Constance is at the orphanage?"

Sarah nodded.

"Thank you," Constance appreciated as Sarah closed the door.

Constance proceeded to the orphanage, her final destination. She'd known some girls and boys her own age that lived there from school. Constance turned to the three-story building, lit up with two lights on either side of the front door. She stepped up onto the platform and gently knocked on the door.

A smiling woman answered her knock. "Yes?"

"Hi, um…" she didn't know what to say. "I'm here because…my father beats me fiercely for no reason." She burst into tears.

The woman led her inside. "Come in, dear."

It was late. Abby told Billy she was going to act now. They talked over their plan once more and Abby was off, praying to God every step of the way. She approached the front desk, where, sure enough, the same guard as the other night, sat, sleeping.

"Excuse me," Abby said, raising her voice to wake him up. Her cloak was off now and she looked like a midnight goddess, as Billy had put it.

The prison was shaped as a circle. In the entrance, you could go either left or right, meeting back where you started if you walked all the way around. The guard woke up with a grumble, talking to himself. When he opened his eyes to see Abby, he sat right up. "Yes, pretty girl?"

Abby smiled. "Hi."

He grinned. "Hi, what can I do for you?"

"I need to speak with Billy Sanson again."

"Property claims?" he questioned.

"Yes," Abby said in an innocent tone.

"All right," the man said, retrieving his keys from the wall where others were stored.

The guard led Abby to Billy's new cell. "Here you go, ma'am."

Abby smiled appreciatively. "Thank you." The guard stood there, then realized he needed to watch the front, as Abby had suggested the first night they had met.

"Okay," Abby whispered. "Be quiet, so no one sees you and starts to cause trouble."

Billy nodded. Abby waited for another minute to go by and then left Billy's cell. He crept out silently as she left.

Abby went to the front. "Oh, pretty girl, are you done?" Abby nodded. "Well, I need to close the cell. Hold on," he started to leave.

Abby walked around the desk he stood behind. She put her hands on his chest, motioning for him to sit down. "No…"

"Uh-huh…" he tried to get away, but the temptation was too much.

"Don't worry about anything. Leave all your problems behind. You're with me now," she said, trying to be seductive.

She guessed it had worked.

The man in charge of the prison's security closed his eyes, puckering up. Abby closed her own eyes, moving in to kiss him. She felt disgusted. Before their lips met, Abby opened her eyes and she saw Billy sneak by, free of prison.

Abby pulled away when Billy was out of sight. "I'm sorry," she rushed to get off of him. "I need to go."

The man frowned. "Goodbye, pretty girl."

"Bye," she smiled, running out the building, knowing too well that she was good and that Billy and her, together, tricked the world, as it had seemed.

Chapter 16

January 9, 1878

> *Billy is finally out of prison. I helped him escape. I know I did something against the law, but after Billy's sentencing, I don't believe in the law as much anymore. I know the sheriff along with the Cotters will come and take him back. But before the Cotters come with the police, I fear they'll come alone. I fear they'll try to do something to us. But that is only a thought. Perhaps it won't be true.*

> *Abby*

"Abby! We did it! I'm out!" Billy exclaimed, lifting her into his arms. They were by the river. The moon was shining brightly on their faces. He put her down. She took his face in her hands and looked at him with loving eyes.

She kissed him and never wanted to let him go. "I'm so happy," she whispered in his ear, hugging him.

Billy smiled. "Me too." He paused for a second, just staring at her. "Come on. Let's go home."

Abby took the night in. It was exciting, being a runaway with Billy. They drifted down the familiar river and Abby watched the stars from where she sat. Billy just stared at her.

"Thank you," he said.

Abby looked away from the dark sky to Billy, smiling. "For what?"

"For always being there. And not running away."

"I'd never run away. You know that," she assured.

When they arrived at the rock, Billy helped Abby out of the canoe as he had always done. "Home at last," Billy sighed. They stood on the rock, hand in hand.

They both wished for summer, which would allow them to dive in the river.

"Come on, Abby. Let's go home."

The next day, Abby strolled Main Street, heading for Jack's home. She was going to stop at his house and then make her way to her own house to fetch Constance.

Abby knocked on the wooden door, waiting patiently for an answer. Jack opened the door, smiling at his cousin. "Hello, Abby. Come in."

"Thank you," she replied as she entered the humble home.

When they were inside, she began: "Billy's home. I just wanted you to know that."

"Abby, that's great."

She chuckled. "Yeah, that's all I wished to tell you."

"Oh…um…Constance…she stopped by last night."

Abby was shocked; surprised she had. "Really?"

Jack nodded. "Yeah, um…she wanted me to tell you she was at the orphanage in town."

"Oh, okay. Thank you. I have to go now. I need to see her." Abby went for the door.

"I'll come by tonight, if you don't mind."

As Abby turned the doorknob, she smiled at the good idea. "That would be nice. Goodbye."

Abby trotted out the door, and headed for Constance. Why was she at the orphanage?

The three-story building stood before Abby when she approached it ten minutes later. She knocked on the door, waiting again for the second time that day for someone to answer. Finally, the owner's daughter, Hope, swung open the door.

"Hello," Hope greeted.

"Hi, um…is Constance Cotter here?"

"You are?"

"I am her older sister, Abby."

"Ah, yes. Constance is expecting you." Hope turned and motioned to Abby to come in.

After Abby closing the large, oak door, Hope led Abby to apparently where some of the girls slept. The room definitely resembled a girl's bedroom. Pink flowers covered the wall. The six beds had nice, soft covers on them. The orphanage seemed like a better home than what they were used to would ever be.

Five girls, around Constance's age, were in the bedroom, braiding each other's hair. One of the girls was Constance.

"Constance?" Hope called after her. Constance looked up to see Abby standing in the doorway. She ran over to her.

"Hi," Constance gasped.

"Hi," Abby responded. "Could we speak alone?" Abby asked Hope.

She nodded. "Certainly." Hope went back downstairs.

"Why did you come here?" Abby asked her younger sister.

Constance sighed. "Because he was going to beat me again. I can't take it anymore. I'm much happier here anyway."

"Really?" Abby was glad to hear that. "I can bring you back to Billy's if you want to."

Constance shook her head. "It's okay. You do whatever you have to do."

Abby kissed Constance on the forehead. "Okay. Maybe I'll see you tomorrow."

Constance replied, "Maybe."

"All right. Well, I must leave now."

"Bye," Constance called after her sister.

Abby was relieved to know Constance was safe and happy. She left the orphanage with a smile on her face.

"Abby!" someone shouted as she started to walk toward Billy's house. Abby turned to see Nick running after her. *He's probably wondering where Christina is*, Abby thought.

"Do you have an idea where Christina and Laura are?" he panted, approaching her.

Abby felt guilty and sorry for him. She sighed, knowing she had to tell him. "Laura is safe. I brought her to Henry's."

He was mystified. "Why did you do that?"

"Because…"

"Is Christina hurt?"

Abby shook her head in reply. "She left."

"Left? To go where?"

She shook her head again. "I don't know…when you left, she told me she couldn't take it anymore, so she had to run away."

He was speechless. "Run away?"

"She just handed me Laura and left. I don't know where she went. I'm sorry." He looked elsewhere, still unable to talk. "I'm sorry, Nick."

He walked away, not saying one word to Abby. She continued her way to Billy's house, putting Christina and Nick aside, and was happier than ever.

It was sunset of the same day. Abby had just finished making dinner, which consisted of pork and mashed potatoes along with jarred carrots from the year before. She also found wine in the shed and Abby decided that it was the right occasion to drink it.

Abby and Billy rocked in their chairs in front of the blazing fire. There was a knock at the door.

"I'll answer it," Billy said sternly and cautiously. He approached the door and put his hand on the brass knob. "Who is it?" he called.

"Jack and Sarah," the visitors answered.

Billy opened the door and sighed at the sight of his friends. "Come in," he invited.

"Mmm…" Jack groaned. "It sure does smell good in here."

Abby walked to the guests and greeted them. "I'm so glad you both could come."

"Thank you for having us," Sarah said.

"No Katherine tonight?" Abby wondered.

"No…she is visiting my aunt for the night."

"Oh."

"Well, come in," Billy told them. "Dinner is hot and I am truly hungry."

The four friends went into the dining room and ate all they could eat. They talked and they laughed, everyone knew it was too good to be perfect. Everyone knew nothing would be the same ever again.

It was sad, given the thought that these people knew how their lives would end up. Tragedy. Someone would have his or her heart broken by the end of the week. And everyone knew whom.

When dinner was done, Jack and Billy sat in the parlor talking about the old times. Sarah and Abby cleaned up the kitchen, and everything was right.

When the women were done, Abby offered to show Sarah Billy's parents' bedroom. To show how gorgeous it was.

"Wow!" gasped Sarah, when Abby swung the door open.

"Isn't it marvelous?" Abby asked.

"Yes, it is."

Downstairs, another knock was at the door. Jack and Billy didn't panic, but were hesitant on knowing what to do. "Hide, Billy," Jack whispered, walking to the door.

When Billy was out of sight, Jack opened the front door and saw the murderers of Gregory and Elizabeth Sanson. "Can I help you?" Jack asked.

"Billy Sanson. We're looking for him," Charles stammered.

"Don't know who you be talkin' about," Jack replied, casually.

"I think you're lyin', boy. Let us in!" Charles began to become impatient.

"No, sir. Do you have a warrant?"

Charles lifted his shotgun to Jack's face. "Is this good enough?" Jack shook his head. "Nope."

"Let us in!" raged Charles. He then knocked Jack over the head with his weapon. Jack fell lifelessly to the ground. The two murderers climbed the stairs to search Billy's bedroom.

"Did you hear that?" Sarah asked Abby when she heard a thump.

"No," Abby shook her head.

"I wonder what's happened." Sarah curiously opened the door

and went to the top of the staircase. She saw Jack lying at the bottom. "Abby! Come quick!"

Before Abby could emerge, Charles Cotter was out of the bedroom across the hall, and he had pushed Sarah down the stairs. Her scream shattered the world.

Abby saw Sarah fall and looked at the man she called her father for so long. "Murderer," she hissed with hatred.

Abby descended from the second story quickly, running after Sarah. She was pregnant and she needed help. She screamed with horror and pain.

Billy came out of hiding to see what was the matter, but the murderers caught him before he could find out what had happened.

The murderers exited the house, with grins on their faces, knowing how revenge smelled.

Abby tried to comfort Sarah the best she could. Jack had finally come to his senses and realized what had happened. They carried Sarah to the canoe to bring her to her father.

The baby was at risk.

Three hours later, Doctor Bridge came out of his office to tell the dreadful news to Jack and Abby. "Is she all right?" Jack asked, hoping and praying she was.

Doctor Bridge began to sob. "Sarah's all right, but your baby…"

Jack sat from where he stood. "No…no…" He cried silently.

"There were complications…I'm so sorry, Jack."

"I'm sorry, too," Abby whispered.

Jack looked up at his father-in-law. "Could I see her?"

Doctor Bridge nodded. "Of course."

Sarah was still and in shock when Jack entered. Endless tears ran down her face. "I'm sorry," she sniffled. "I'm so sorry."

Jack walked to his wife. "It's not your fault, Sarah. It's that bastard's fault. He will pay, Sarah. I promise you."

Chapter 17

January 11, 1878

> *Charles Cotter has murdered yet another innocent human being. Sarah's baby is dead and it's because of that awful man.*
> *Now Billy is back in prison too. I am guessing it will be best if I leave and never return.*
> *I need answers.*

> *Abby*

Sarah was lying in her bed, sleeping. Jack watched her as small tears tumbled down from his eyes. Abby knocked softly on the door and let herself in. She brought hot tea for Jack as well as Sarah for when she would wake.

"Her father says she might not be able to have children anymore," Jack whispered, trying to understand the fact.

Abby stopped before leaving. "I'm so sorry."

Jack spoke once more. "And it's the fault of that man. He pushed her down. How did you become so kind living with such awful people?"

"I don't know. I think it's because of Billy. He's the one who I really lived with. In my heart, at least."

Jack nodded.

"I'm going to visit Billy. I will be back." She left the room quietly, trying not to disturb the sleepiness in the air.

Abby sauntered to the familiar building where Billy was being held prisoner. She went to the front desk and asked to speak with Billy for this was the last time she'd ever see him.

The security guard granted her wish and led Abby to his cell. He opened the door with one of the many keys he held.

"Abby!" Billy said, going to her when she entered to room.

"I'm sorry!" she sobbed, holding him.

"It's okay."

She shook her head. "No, it's not. Tomorrow…I'm leaving. The day after tomorrow you will pay your sentence."

Billy let go of Abby and frowned, sitting back down on his bed. "This is the last time, isn't it?"

Abby looked away.

"Isn't it, Abby?" he whispered.

She nodded, trying to keep her tears inside. Billy stood up and walked to Abby, embracing her. "I love you," he said softly.

She looked up at him with watery eyes. "Billy, don't. Don't make it harder than it already is. Please…I can't deal with this."

"You need to be strong. Be strong for everyone."

She collapsed in the cell. Abby sat on the floor in complete misery, wishing the world would come to an end.

"I can't!" she cried. "I can't! Not now! Not ever!" she shouted so loud, everyone in the prison could hear.

"Ma'am, you need to leave now," the guard told her, unlocking the door.

"No!" she screamed. "Not yet!"

"Abby, go," Billy whispered. He hugged her again and in her ear, he said softly, "I love you, Abby."

She looked at him with large eyes, unable to say anything back to him. "Come on, ma'am."

She sobbed all the way back to the Cotter General Store. She was going to pack all her belongings and spend her last night at Jack's house.

Abby held her head high as she meandered to her bedroom. She noticed all of Constance's belongings were gone.

Abby put all of her dresses in her trunk. She had not much to bring with her. Memories would only make her cry in Boston.

She wanted to bring her rocking chair, which Billy made her, but it was impossible.

Everything seemed impossible.

Abby pulled her diary from under her cot. She shuffled through the pages, remembering every journal entry she made. She had started it because Billy was gone and she had no one else to talk to.

Her next stop was Old Mann Rock where she would bury her diary next to Billy's parents, along with Gregory's journal and Elizabeth's poem, "My Sunshine."

She made one last entry in the pages. Abby wrote:

January 11, 1878

This will be my last journal entry. This journal has come to an end as well as my story. My story that all began with Old Mann Rock.

Thank you for being there for me.

Love,
Abby

Abby wiped away her last tear and stuffed her book in her trunk.

She dug in the dirt with her fingernails to make a hole big enough for her diary and the Sansons' things. "Goodbye," she whispered, patting the dirt smooth over the hole.

Abby went to the rock and watched the water flowing about. Then she looked up at the rope, which hung loosely from the arm of the great oak tree.

She looked back down in the water. She remembered the first time she jumped from the rock. She had been so frightened. It brought a smile to her face.

Abby wondered what kind of life she would had if she never had met Billy. But then she shrugged the thought away and reminded herself of all the pain their relationship had endured. It was all worth it.

Abby knew it was time to leave because it was sunset, the last sunset she would ever see on the rock.

Old Mann Rock had been her home since she was ten years of age. It seemed like so very long ago. "Goodbye, Old Mann," Abby said, kissing her hand and then placing it on the cold surface of the rock.

She stood up and climbed down from the peak. Abby looked back at her home, realizing for the first time she wouldn't just miss Billy, she'd miss all the memories the rock gave her.

Abby arrived at Jack's house an hour after the sun went down. She had her trunk beside her.

Jack answered Abby's knock and helped her bring her trunk in.

"How is Sarah feeling?" Abby asked, concerned.

"She's getting better."

"That's good to hear."

Abby could see in Jack's face and his tone that he was stressed out. He needed to rest. "Jack, I think you should go to bed," Abby suggested.

Jack thought a while and then looked at Abby. "Maybe you're right." He searched around the house with his eyes, and then looked back at Abby. "I'm sorry, Abby, we had no going away party or anything for you," he apologized.

Abby smiled. "The least I would want is a celebration for my leaving. A good night sleep, that's all I need. That's what you need too."

"I guess so," he smiled, drowsily. "Katherine is in her bedroom. You can sleep with her if you want."

"Thank you," Abby said. Jack turned and left to go to his bedroom.

Abby went to Katherine's bedroom and knocked on the door slowly.

"Come in," she replied. Abby let herself in.

Katherine was at her bureau, fumbling through different things on the top of it. She was dressed in her nightgown and her hair was brushed.

"Hi," Abby greeted.

"Hi, Abby," she said back, not taking her eyes off of what she handled.

"Jack said I could sleep in your room tonight."

"Oh, yes, that'll be fine." She was still occupied with something she held.

"What do you have there?" Abby questioned.

Katherine brought her treasure to Abby so she could see it. "A baby mouse."

Abby screeched at the sight of the small, helpless animal. "Oh, it's so small."

"I don't think she'll make it," Katherine said. The tiny mouse was no bigger than a pointer finger.

"Poor thing."

"Yeah. I'm hoping overnight she won't die." Katherine set the miniature animal in a box on her dresser. "I'm going to bed." She went to her bed and climbed in. Abby did the same. "Abby, why are you leaving?" Katherine asked, softly. "Don't you like us anymore?"

"Of course I do. I just have to, I guess."

"Why aren't you going to marry Billy?"

"Because…he's been sentenced to death, Katherine, and there's nothing I can do about it." She seemed mad and upset. The tone of her voice frightened Katherine.

"Oh." The thirteen-year-old girl turned to face the window, letting a tear free. Her best friend in the world was leaving.

It was the day Abby would leave the only place she ever knew. She was going somewhere new, larger, and full of strangers.

Tomorrow Billy would be hung for the town to watch. Maybe it was better she was leaving the day before instead of the actual day. She feared it wouldn't be possible to leave and let go.

Let go of him.

Let go of Billy.

Abby prepared to go and say goodbye to Constance. It would be one of the most difficult things she had to do. But it had to be done.

And she dreaded doing it every minute of it.

Abby walked onto Main Street and observed the Vermont nature for what she thought would be the last day. The sky was partly cloudy and there was a hint of a breeze in the winter air.

She took it all in and continued her stroll to her sister's goodbye.

Abby knocked on the heavy door, and Hope, answered it graciously. Hope fetched Constance, and then Abby followed her younger sister to the back garden.

Although it was winter, the garden seemed alive. But that was impossible. Constance was in melancholy when she saw Abby. Abby understood that Constance knew why she had come.

Constance's head fell. "You're not leaving, are you?" A tear fell from her eyes.

Abby nodded. "Yeah."

Constance sniffled, trying to keep everything in. Abby did the same.

"It's not fair, Abby," Constance sobbed, lifting her head to stare at her sister with water-filled eyes.

"What's not?" Abby looked away.

"You leaving. Abby, you're the nicest person I know and you don't deserve this. Not at all."

Abby looked back at Constance. "Sometimes…well, everyone has different lives. And sometimes people like us, the good people lose…the bad people are just destined to win. But they pay in the end. It's the luck we need to pray for, Constance." Abby held her grieving sister. "I know everything will work out for you, though."

"How do you know?"

"You're strong. You're smart. You know what's right and what's wrong."

"Really? You believe it, Abby? You really believe I am?"

Abby nodded and wiped away one of Constance's tears. "You're everything I want to be."

Constance smiled and hugged Abby tightly. " You are just the same! Abby, oh, Abby, you are!"

"Thank you, Constance."

Abby stood, followed by Constance. "I must go."

Constance hugged her sister for the last time. "I love you, Abby. Good luck. Don't forget to write me."

"I love you, too. I will, don't worry." Abby turned and left, wiping her lonely tears.

Abby opened the door to Jack's house and knew there was panic in the room. Jack came into the room panting.

"Good, you're here," Jack said. "Sarah's having problems. I need to go fetch her father. He went to a clinic out of town. I know where he is. Could I borrow Rosie?"

"Sure you can," Abby replied.

"Please don't leave until I get back," he said, running out to get Sarah's father.

Abby went to Sarah's bedroom. Katherine was holding her hand and she was sweating and in pain. "Sarah?" Abby called.

"Oh, Abby!" Sarah cried. "Stop the pain! Please!"

"I'm sorry. I can't." Abby rushed to Sarah's side. "But is there anything I can get you?"

Sarah shook her head, breathed heavily, and shut her eyes tight. "Where's Jack?"

"He left to find your father," Abby informed.

Sarah finally calmed down. She told them the pain was fading, but she was sure it would return.

Katherine told Abby that her baby mouse had lived through the night. Katherine felt it was a sign of hope.

Abby had faith that it was.

"Abby, are you leaving today?" Sarah questioned.

"I'm supposed to, but I don't think I will. I don't want to leave you."

"Oh," Sarah apologized, very dreary. "You don't have to stay. I'm sorry to ruin your plans."

Abby smiled. "Don't be silly, Sarah. The longer I stay, the happier I am."

"That's…" Sarah couldn't finish her sentence. Pain shot all around her body like hundreds of knives piercing her skin at once.

Abby took hold of Sarah's left hand. Sarah clutched onto it with a firm grasp. She screamed out, crying, for the pain was too much to bear.

Abby felt so horrible. It was the Cotters' fault. All their fault. If only...

No.

Abby didn't think of the possible ifs. She didn't look to the past. Instead she would seek the present and the future.

What would happen to Sarah? Why did this innocent young wife need to suffer such consequences?

She remembered what she had told Constance earlier that day. *Sometimes the bad people are destined to win.* Did she really believe in her own philosophy on life? She couldn't think of it. She didn't want her words to become the truth.

Eventually, Sarah fell into a deep sleep, which gave Katherine and Abby a moment to breath. Abby grabbed her cloak. "I'll be back as soon as possible. I'm going to tell Nick we can't leave until tomorrow."

"You're not?" Katherine's face lit up.

"No," she smiled. Abby realized that saying goodbye to Katherine would be as hard as saying goodbye to Constance. "I'll be back."

Abby gently knocked on Nick's door. He answered.

"Abby? You're not ready?" Nick asked, noticing she was in her everyday dress.

"Nick..." she said softly. "Could we leave...say tomorrow?"

"Abby," he shrugged, obviously angry.

"Please. Sarah, Jack's wife is having problems. Jack went to get the doctor. I can't leave her."

He sighed. She wondered why this was such a conflict in his mind. "We'll leave early tomorrow morning. I promise you."

Nick said: "Fine." Then he closed the door on his wife-to-be with no further words. Abby put Nick away in her head for a moment and thought of her first priority, Sarah.

Sarah was still sleeping when Jack and her father arrived later that night. Abby was relieved to see the sight of them. She didn't want Sarah to wake and be in more pain.

Doctor Bridge woke his daughter gently. "Daddy?" she whispered.

"Yes," the older man replied.

"What's happened to me?"

He shook his head. "I don't know, my dear."

"I am hurting. Where the baby used to lay."

"I understand."

"Could you make it better?" she pleaded.

"Sarah, you will just have to let this pass. There is nothing I can do. I'm sorry."

Sarah took a deep breath and turned to her husband who held her hand, smiling. "Jack."

"I missed you."

"So did I. Don't leave me anymore. Please?"

"Don't you worry." Sarah closed her eyes and went into a deep sleep. She was peaceful for the rest of the night.

Chapter 18

It was the thirteenth of January, the day of Billy Sanson's hanging. The men of the town were setting up the gallows down at the port, in the middle of the street.

Abby was in front of the fireplace in Jack's humble home, situating her trunk. She was miserably unhappy.

Jack entered the room, carrying something small in his hand. "I'll help you to Nick's."

"Thank you," Abby smiled.

Jack sat beside her. "I have something for you."

"That's not necessary. I didn't get anything for you."

"It's not really from me. It was your mother's. Somehow, the night of her wedding she left it here. My mother always wanted to give it to you, but she never had the chance." Jack opened his hand. Inside, was a gold ring. It was tarnished a bit, but nevertheless, it was beautiful. There was an inscription. It read: "I will love you forever."

"It's beautiful," she said, letting a tear free.

"It was her wedding ring," Jack informed.

"Thank you." Abby hugged her cousin.

"You look lovely," he complimented. Abby wore a new dress. It was navy blue and came with a white hat. "You will fit in well with the Boston society."

"I hope."

"I wish for you to remember you fit in best here, though."

"I won't ever forget."

Katherine came into the room, weeping. She immediately hugged Abby. "Please don't leave."

"I'm sorry," Abby apologized.

Katherine cried deeply in Abby's arms. "You don't have to be. It's not your fault."

"But it is, in a way," Abby said.

"Don't blame yourself," Katherine sniffled, holding her cousin harder.

Sarah was still asleep when Abby went to say goodbye. Instead of waking her, she wrote her a letter.

January 13, 1878

Sarah,

Today I am leaving this lovely town and moving to Boston, Massachusetts. I did not want to wake you, for I did not want you to wake in pain.

I wish I could turn back the time and make everything better, but I am sorry that that is not possible.

You have become one of my best friends in the world and I wish you and Jack the best of luck.

You two are so sincere. I envy what you have. You have love for each other and I know that your love can accomplish all obstacles such as ones you are experiencing now. My love goes out to all of you. I will write.

Love Always,
Abby

Jack set Abby's trunk down in front of Nick's house. He then held Abby with all his might. "I love you," he whispered to her.

"I love you, too," Abby replied, trying to hold her tears back. "I will write as soon as I get there."

"Okay. Good luck, Abby. Whenever you want to come home, there's always a place for you to stay."

"I will keep that in mind. Thank you for the ring."

"You're most welcome."

"Bye, Jack," Abby whispered.

"Goodbye."

Abby turned and climbed the stoop to meet Nick. Jack went back to his house. Nick answered and smiled. "You look beautiful."

"Thank you." Abby went inside and Nick grabbed her trunk.

"We'll leave in about a half hour. Is that all right?" Nick asked.

"Sure," Abby said, trying to sound happy.

"You're going to love Boston, Abby. It's totally different than this. Much more civilized."

"I can't wait," she replied.

Nick went into his bedroom and returned with an armful of his belongings. He continued into another room. On his way, he dropped a book.

Abby picked up the book and realized it was his journal. She rummaged through it, even though she knew it was wrong to spy on his personal thoughts. She went to the last page and read:

January 13, 1878

This is the last page of my journal, but the start of a new beginning. This started with a night with Abby and now I am marrying her. Goodbye.

Abby went to the first page of his book. She read:

September 18, 1877

Tonight I innocently got Abby intoxicated. I brought her to my house and...well, you know. I didn't know what to do with her. I put her in an alleyway. Was that wrong?

Abby was furious. She was in rage. He lied to her. He lied to her all along. But wait...

He was the one who...

She broke down crying, wondering why she had ever doubted he would do such awful things. She screamed. Nick rushed into the room. "Abby! What's wrong?"

Abby stood up and pointed her finger at him, sobbing at the same time. "You!" she screamed. "You!"

"What?" he asked, naive. "What did I do?"

"You know what very well you did! You're disgusting! I am disgusted!" She showed him his journal. "You raped me, Nick!"

His eyes grew large.

"Don't be shocked! You know you did!"

"Abby, calm down!"

"Calm down? Calm down? Why should I calm down when you're the one who…How could you do that to me? How could you lie to me like that?"

"Come on, Abby. Let's go."

"Are you out of your mind? You think I'm going to marry you? You're a fool!"

"Abby…don't."

She went to her trunk and went out the door with it.

"Abby!" he called after her.

She slammed the door behind her.

She carried her heavy trunk through the street raging and thinking of what to do next. "Excuse me?" Abby asked a man in the street passing her by. "When is Billy Sanson sentenced to be hung?"

"At two o'clock, ma'am," he replied.

"Thank you." They went their separate ways.

Abby remembered it was about half past twelve. She had read it on Nick's clock. She quickly thought of a plan. She hope to God it would work. Abby would need Jack's help and she had no doubts that he wouldn't.

Abby climbed Old Mann Rock, running because time was so important. She rushed to Billy's house. Inside she grabbed things she would need for her plan.

Abby sprinted back to Jack's house and barged through the door. They only had an hour.

"Abby?" Jack was surprised. "Why are you here?"

"He was the one who raped me," Abby said, not crying, but trying to stay strong.

Jack went to her and held her. "I'm sorry."

"I'm not marrying him."

"Good, Abby. Good for you."

"I need your help though. We have less than an hour to get him."

"Get who?"

"Billy."

"Abby, you can't! The police will just find him again."

"Not if we leave town."

"Are you sure?"

Abby nodded. "Positive."

"Okay. Let's get Rosie ready. We'll leave her nearby so you can easily get her."

It was about fifteen minutes before two o'clock in the afternoon. Jack and Abby made their way to the gallows. They stashed Rosie in an alleyway where she waited for Abby.

A crowd of people suffocated the stage. Jack and Abby did the same.

Abby hugged Jack for what she knew would be the last time until they would meet again. "Good luck," Jack whispered.

Chapter 19

Ten minutes later, Billy clambered onto the gallows. Abby prayed for his life. She took a deep breath for what she was about to do was highly unbelievable to her. They slipped the noose around his neck.

"Wait!" she yelled. Everyone stopped and looked at her.

Billy smiled in relief.

Jack and Abby made their way to the front of the crowd. Abby was shaking, for she was scared.

"I'm sorry," she apologized to the crowd. "I just need to thank the people that brought Billy Sanson to justice...my parents. Can they come up please?"

Jack and Abby climbed the stairs to stand next to Billy. Sure enough, the Cotters came to join them.

Jack said, "Thank you so very much."

"It was nothing," Charles said, frowning in disbelief of Abby's gratitude.

"So, Daddy...who did Billy murder?"

"Tom Marshall. A very good friend of mine," Charles told the crowd.

"Why?" Abby inquired.

"I don't know."

"Well, Billy never left his home. Were you at his house, Daddy?"

"Yes."

"Why?"

"Because we had negotiating to do."

"Negotiating? You mean to finish him off because you already had murdered his parents eight years earlier. Didn't you?"

He looked innocent. "What do you mean, Abby?"

"She means you killed Elizabeth and Gregory Sanson because Gregory turned you in, didn't you?" Jack asked, as Abby jumped from the stage.

193

"No," he replied.

"And you pushed my beautiful wife down the stairs. Did you know she was pregnant? Did you know we are suffering the loss of our child?" Jack raged.

"What are you talking about, young man?" Cecile butted in.

"You both are murderers."

The crowd began wailing different emotions. Some angry. Some in shock.

"Admit it! You know it is the truth! Admit that you murdered Gregory and Elizabeth Sanson."

The sheriff came to them. "Let it rest, boy. If he says he didn't, then he didn't."

"Wait! Don't you remember eight years ago the Cotter General Store was about to go out of business? The Sansons were going to purchase it because the Cotters were going to be evicted. Well, is it called the Sanson General Store? No, it is still called the Cotter General Store. What ever happened to the Sansons, you wonder? They were murdered because of revenge!"

"Is that true, Charles?" the sheriff asked.

"Of course not!" he was in a fury.

"Yes it is," Jack pushed.

The crowd yelled their rage out to Charles. "Fine!" the murderer shouted.

The crowd went silent.

"I did! I murdered them! I enjoyed every moment of it too!" Cecile began to run. "And oh, your wench," Charles said to Jack, "too bad. She was a nice one!" Charles then ran after his wife.

Jack's fury bottled up inside of him. He chased them, as did the sheriff.

Abby rode on Rosie in the crowd. She hopped off of her and pulled a knife from under skirt to cut Billy free.

"You came?"

"Of course I did," she said.

Billy and Abby jumped onto Rosie. They rode off to the Connecticut River, knowing everything would work out after all.

Chapter 20

Billy and Abby slept under the stars on the banks of the Connecticut. They decided to stop and see Liz and then head west.

"I love you, Billy," Abby whispered, not knowing he was awake.

"I love you, too."

"You're awake?"

"Have been."

"Oh."

"It feels good to be alive."

"It sure does."

They held hands for the rest of the night, knowing that this was a perfect ending to their story of struggle.

"We'll need to go back," Abby said, as they strode on Rosie. "In a few months or years, of course. I told Jack to hold our chairs for us."

"You did?"

"Yes."

"You're wonderful."

"As are you."

Abby changed her thinking on life. She decided the good people win. She decided that they have to go through heartbreak and lies to get what they want. They sometimes even had to give up something they loved. For Abby and Billy's case, it was their true home, Old Mann Rock.

The two waited before Liz's front door before knocking. Billy could not pass Enfield and not visit the woman that had taken him in months before. Billy looked at Abby and smiled, finally knocking on the door.

Liz answered and looked at Billy, a sudden grin appearing on her face. "Now…you must be Abby."

Printed in the United States
17738LVS00002B/259-324